Richard Marsh

The Woman with One Hand (and) Mr. Ely's Engagement

CW00552067

Richard Marsh

The Woman with One Hand (and) Mr. Ely's Engagement

1st Edition | ISBN: 978-3-75241-664-0

Place of Publication: Frankfurt am Main, Germany

Year of Publication: 2020

Outlook Verlag GmbH, Germany.

THE WOMAN WITH ONE HAND

AND

Mr. Ely's Engagement

BY

RICHARD MARSH

CHAPTER I

It caught my eye at once. When a man is dining off his last half-crown he is apt to have his eyes wide open. Having just disposed of a steak which, under the circumstances, did not seem to be so large as it might have been, I picked up a paper which, as he had laid it down, the diner in front appeared to have done with. As it was folded, the agony column stared me in the face. And among the "agonies" was this:—

"If James Southam, at one time of Dulborough, will apply to the undersigned, he will hear of something to his advantage.—Messrs. Cleaver and Caxton, Solicitors, Thirteen, Bacup Street, London, S.E."

Now, I am James Southam, at one time of Dulborough, but, although I do answer to that description, a very clear something told me that if I did hear of anything to my advantage by applying to anybody, then the age of miracles was not yet done with. Still, as, when a man has spent on a doubtful meal one-and-sevenpence out of his last half-crown, something to his advantage is exactly what he wants to hear of, I clipped that advertisement out of the paper under the waiter's nose, and put it in my waistcoat pocket.

On referring to a directory in a convenient post-office, I found that Bacup Street was in the neighbourhood of the Old Kent Road. That did not seem to be a promising address, and, so far as appearances went, it fulfilled its promise. It struck me that Bacup Street, speaking generally, looked more than a trifle out at elbows, and Number Thirteen seemed to be the shabbiest house which it contained. An untidy youth received me. After keeping me waiting for a quarter of an hour in what might have served as an apology for a cupboard, he ushered me into a room beyond. In this inner room there were two men. One was seated at a table, the other was standing with his hat at the back of his head in front of the empty fireplace. They looked at me, then they looked at each other; and, unless I am mistaken, they exchanged a glance of surprise. The man at the table addressed me, without evincing any desire to rise.

"Well, sir, and what can we do for you?"

"That," I said, "is what I want to know."

The man smiled, as if he was not quite sure that there was anything to

2

smile at. I took the newspaper cutting out of my waistcoat pocket.

"I have just seen this advertisement. I am James Southam, at one time of Dulborough, and if you are Messrs. Cleaver and Caxton, I have come to you to hear of something to my advantage."

For some moments my words remained unanswered. They both stared at me as if they were endeavouring by mere force of visual inspection to find out what sort of person I really was. Then the man at the table spoke again.

"Of course you have evidence as to the truth of what you say?"

"I have my card in my pocket; here are letters which have been addressed to me. If you will tell me what I am going to hear of to my advantage I will place you in the way of obtaining a sufficiency of any sort of evidence you may require."

I placed a card on the table, and some old envelopes, having first of all taken out the letters. The two men forgathered. They examined my "documents." They spoke to each other in whispers. Holding out one of the envelopes, the man who had already spoken pointed with a stubby and unclean first finger to the address which was on the front of it.

"Is this your present address?"

"No; at present I have no address."

"What do you mean?"

"I have been presented with the key of the street."

"Do you mean that you are impecunious?"

"I do."

The individual with the hat on who had not yet spoken to me, spoke to me now, with a decidedly unpleasant grin. "Stone-broke?" he said.

I did not like to turn myself inside-out to strangers, especially to such strangers: but I had recently had to do a good many things which I had not liked. Above all, I had begun to realise the truth of the adage which tells us that beggars must not be choosers.

"I am as nearly stone-broke as a man can be who is in possession of a fair variety of pawn-tickets, the clothes he stands up in, and elevenpence in cash."

There was some further whispering between the pair, then the individual with the hat on addressed me again.

"If you will step outside, in a few minutes we will speak to you again."

I stepped outside. They kept me outside longer than I altogether relished.

I was on the point of, at all hazards, asserting my dignity, when the man with the hat on, opening the door of the inner office, invited me to enter. It was he, when I entered, who took up the conversation.

"We are not, you must understand, at liberty to furnish you with particulars of the matter referred to in our advertisement without first of all communicating with our client."

"Who is your client?"

"That, without having received permission, we cannot tell you either. Can you not guess?"

The fellow stared at me in a manner which I instinctively resented. His glance conveyed a meaning which seemed to be the reverse of flattering.

"I certainly cannot guess, nor have I the least intention of trying. I have the pleasure of wishing you good-day."

I turned to go; the fellow stopped me.

"One moment! Where are you off to?" I turned to him again. This time he was eyeing me with what I felt was an insolent grin. "For a man in the position in which you say you are you don't seem over anxious to hear of something to your advantage."

"Nor do you seem over anxious to tell it me."

"We are solicitors, man, not principals. It is our business to act on the instructions we have received. Listen to me." I listened. "We have reason to believe that our client would desire to be acquainted with your address, so that he may be able to place himself in immediate communication with you, should you turn out to be the James Southam he is in search of. As you don't appear, at present, to have an address of your own, we are willing to provide you with one."

"Explain yourself."

"We will take you to an hotel, and we will guarantee your reasonable expenses there until you hear from us again. Should you not turn out to be the required James Southam, we will pay your bill, withdraw our guarantee, and there will be an end of the matter, so far as we are concerned. You will have received some advantage, at any rate."

I accepted the proposition. When the sum of elevenpence stands between a man and starvation he is apt not to be over particular in picking holes in proffered offers of board and lodging. The untidy youth fetched a cab. The individual with the hat on accompanied me in it, there and then, to one of those innumerable private hotels which are found in the side streets off the Strand. He went inside, while I waited for him in the cab. When he reappeared he fetched me in, introduced me to a tall, thin woman, whom he called Mrs. Barnes, drew me aside, told me that he had made all arrangements, that I should hear from him again, and that, in the meantime, I should find myself all right. Then he went, leaving me in that private hotel, for all I knew to the contrary, a pensioner on his bounty.

CHAPTER II

THE WAITER—AND THE HAND

When I had dined—they gave me for nothing a better dinner than the one I had had in the middle of the day for one-and-sevenpence—the feeling that, to say the least of it, I was in an equivocal position, began to chasten. Instead, I began to feel, as the schoolboys have it, that I was in for a lark. That I really was going to hear, either through Messrs. Cleaver and Caxton, or through anybody else, of something to my advantage, I never for a moment believed. I was an orphan. I had what I take it are the best of reasons for knowing I have not a single living relative. I have no friends: I never had. I was, at my mother's death, employed in an office from which I was shortly after ignominiously ejected, owing to a difference of opinion I was so unfortunate as to have with the senior clerk. I had spent my substance, such as it was, and twelve months, in seeking for other occupation.

My story was a prosaic and a sordid one. That I could hear of something to my advantage, from any source whatever, was an idea I utterly scouted.

I dined alone. The waiter informed me that, for the moment, I was the only visitor in the house. No doubt, under those circumstances, I was welcome. This waiter was a man with iron-grey hair and a pair of curiously big, black eyes; I noticed them as he flitted about the room, but I had much better reason to notice them a little later on. As I rose from the table I gave outspoken utterance to words which were a sort of tag to the sequence of my thoughts—

"Well, James Southam," I exclaimed, "you're in for it at last."

This I said out loud, foolishly, no doubt. The waiter was moving towards the door. He had some plates in his hand; as I spoke, he dropped these plates. They smashed to pieces on the floor. He turned to me as if he turned on a pivot. The fashion of his countenance changed; he glared at me as if I or he had suddenly gone mad. The pupils of his eyes dilated—it was then I realised what curious eyes they were.

"Who the devil are you?" he cried. "How do you know my name's James Southam?"

I do not know how it was, but a splash of inspiration seemed all at once to come to me—I do not know from where.

6

"You are James Southam," I said; "at one time of Dulborough."

I could plainly see that the man was trembling, either with fear or with rage, and it struck me that it was with a mixture of both.

"What has that to do with you?" he gasped.

"It has this to do with me—that I want you."

An empty beer-bottle was on the table. With the rapidity of some frantic wild animal, rushing forward he caught this bottle by the neck, and, before I had realised his intention, he struck me with it on the head. He was a smaller man than I, but, when next I began to take an interest in the things of this world, I was lying on the floor, and the room was empty. My namesake, all the evidence went to show, had felled me like a log, and, without any sort of ceremony, had left me where I fell.

I sat up on the floor, I put my hand to my head. It ached so badly that I could scarcely see out of my eyes. With some difficulty I sprang to my feet. On attaining a more or less upright position I became conscious that the trepidation of my legs inclined me in another direction.

"If this," I told myself, "is hearing of something to my advantage, I've heard enough."

As I endeavoured to obtain support by leaning against the mantelpiece the room door opened, and the tall, thin woman, whom I had been told was Mrs. Barnes, came in.

"I beg your pardon," she began. She looked round the room, then she looked at me. So far as I could judge in the then state of my faculties, she appeared surprised. "I thought the waiter was here."

"He was here."

"How long has he been gone?"

"Some minutes."

"It is very odd! I have been looking for him everywhere. I thought that he was still upstairs with you." She glanced at the ruined crockery. "What has happened?—who has broken the plates?"

"The waiter—he dropped them. He also dropped the bottle."

I did not explain that he had dropped the latter on my head, and almost broken it into as many pieces as the plates.

"It is very careless of him. I must see where he is."

I fancied, from the expression of her face, that she perceived that there was more in the matter than met the eye. But, if so, she did not give audible expression to her perceptions. She left the room, and, when she had gone, I also left the room, and went to bed. I realised that the complications, and, if I may be permitted to say so, the ramifications of the situation, were for the moment beyond my grasp. In the morning I might be able to look the position fairly in the face, but, just then—no! I hastened to put myself between the sheets. Scarcely was I between them than I fell asleep.

I was awakened, as it seemed to me, just after I had fallen asleep, by some one knocking at the bedroom door. The knocking must have startled me out of a dreamless slumber, because it was a moment or two before I could remember where I was. Then I understood that some one was endeavouring to attract my attention from without.

"Who's there?" I said.

"It is I, Mrs. Barnes, the landlady. I wish to speak to you."

"What, now? What time is it? Won't the morning do?

"No, I must speak to you at once."

It seemed that, in my hurry to get into bed, I had forgotten to put the gas out. Slipping into some garments I opened the door. There stood Mrs. Barnes, with a lighted candle in her hand. For some cause or other she was in a state of unmistakable uneasiness. She looked white and haggard.

"I cannot find the waiter," she said.

"You cannot find the waiter!" I stared. "I am sorry to hear it, if you want to find him. But may I ask what that has to do with me?"

"I believe it has a good deal to do with you. What took place between you in the coffee-room?"

"Really, I am not aware that anything took place between us in the coffee-room that was of interest to you."

She came a step forward. Raising the lighted candle, she almost thrust it in my face. She stared at me with strained and eager eyes. She seemed to see something in my face: though what there was to see, except bewilderment, was more than I could guess.

"I don't believe you. You are deceiving me. Did you quarrel with him? Who are you? Tell me! I have a right to know—I am his wife!"

"His wife!" Complications seemed to be increasing. "I thought your name was Barnes."

"So is his name Barnes. What has happened? What do you know about him? Tell me."

"What do I know about him? I know nothing. So far as I am aware, I never saw the man in my life before."

"I don't believe you—you are lying! Where has he gone, and why? You shall tell me—I'll make you!"

She forced her way into the room; in doing so she forced me back. When she was in, she shut the door and stood with her back to it. Her voice had risen to a scream. Her manner almost threatened personal violence. I felt that the hotel to which I had been introduced was conducted on lines with which I had not been hitherto familiar.

"If, as you say, and as I have no reason to doubt, this person is your husband, and he has really disappeared, I can understand that your excitement is not unjustified; but you are mistaken if you suppose that I am in any way to blame. I will tell you exactly what happened between us." I turned aside so that I might have some sort of chance of making up my mind as to how much, on the spur of the moment, it might be advisable to tell her. "Your husband waited on me at dinner. During dinner we scarcely exchanged half a dozen words. After dinner I said something which, although it was spoken out loud, was said to myself, but which affected him in the most extraordinary and unexpected manner."

"What did you say?"

"I said 'I want you.'"

"You said, 'I want you'?" The woman gave a sort of nervous clutch at the door behind her. "Are you a policeman?"

"I am nothing of the kind. You ought to know better than I what your husband has on his conscience. I can only suppose that, for some cause, he stands in terror of the officers of the law; because, no sooner had I innocently uttered what, I believe, is a regular policeman's formula, than, without a word of warning, he caught up the empty bottle which was on the table, like a madman, and knocked me down with it."

"Knocked you down with it!" The woman's face was as white as her own sheets. I saw that she needed the support of the door to aid her stand. "You said nothing to me when I came in."

"I was so astounded by the man's behaviour, and so stunned by his violence, that I was not in a fit state for saying anything. I intended to wait till the morning, and then have it out both with you and with him."

"You are telling me the truth?"

9

"I am."

So I was, though I might not have been telling all of it. I appeared to have told enough of it for her, because immediately afterwards she departed—unless I err, not much easier in her mind because of the visit she had paid to me.

In the morning, as might have been expected, I woke with a headache. I did not feel in the best of health, either physical or mental, when I went down to breakfast. That meal was served by a maidservant. Bringing in a letter on a waiter, she asked if it was for me. As it was addressed to me by name—"Mr. James Southam "—I not only claimed, I opened it. It contained a letter and some enclosures. Here is the letter, word for word:—

"DEAR SIR,—I have just had a telegram from Messrs. Cleaver and Caxton, acquainting me with your address. It gives me great pleasure to write to you. I am just now detained by business, but I hope to call on you at the very earliest opportunity, at latest in the course of a day or two. I assure you that it will be greatly to your advantage. As some slight guarantee of this I beg your acceptance of the enclosed. You need have no fear. You will find in me, in all respects, a friend.

"I will let you know, by telegram, when I am coming. Until then,

"Believe me, your sincere well-wisher,

"DUNCAN ROTHWELL."

The "enclosed" took the shape of four five-pound bank-notes. Who "Duncan Rothwell" was I had not the faintest notion. To me the name was wholly unfamiliar. The letter was neither addressed nor dated. The post-mark on the envelope was Manchester. Messrs. Cleaver and Caxton must have telegraphed so soon as I had left them, and clearly Mr. Rothwell had written immediately on receipt of their wire. The letter was fairly worded, but something about the writing, and indeed about the whole get up of the thing, suggested that it had not been written by a highly educated man—a gentleman.

In any case it seemed sufficiently clear that it was not intended for me, until, fingering the thing, and turning it over and over, I chanced to open the sheet of paper on which it was written. It was a large sheet of business letter-paper. The communication was all contained on the front page, and as there was still plenty of room to spare, it did not occur to me that there could be additions, say, for instance, in the shape of a postscript. It was by the purest chance that my fidgety fingers pulled the sheet wide open. So soon as they had done so I perceived that I was wrong. In the middle of the third page was this:—

"P.S.—It was with great regret that I heard of your mother's lamented death at Putney. I had the melancholy satisfaction of visiting her grave in Wandsworth Cemetery. This will facilitate matters greatly."

Then the letter was intended for me after all. My mother had died at Putney—she had been buried in Wandsworth Cemetery. There might, although I had not been aware of it, have been two James Southams in Dulborough; the coincidence was credible. But it was scarcely credible that the other James Southam's mother could also have died at Putney, and have been buried in Wandsworth Cemetery. Why, or in what sense, my mother's death might facilitate matters, was more than I could say. But, in the face of that postscript, there still seemed sufficient doubt as to which James Southam was about to hear of something to his advantage, to justify me in remaining where I was, and allowing events to take their course.

As I was standing at the window, meditating whether or not I should go for a stroll, the maidservant appeared with a message.

"Mrs. Barnes's compliments, and if you are at liberty, could she speak to you in the private parlour?"

I was not anxious to see Mrs. Barnes. I had a suspicion that if I was not careful I might become more involved than was desirable in her private affairs. Still, if I remained in her house I could scarcely avoid speaking to her. My impulse was to go to Messrs. Cleaver and Caxton, and ask them to shift my quarters. But they might decline, and—well, I shrugged my shoulders, and went and spoke to her.

The private parlour proved to be a small room, and a stuffy one. Mrs. Barnes received me on the threshold. She opened the door to permit me to enter, and having followed me in she shut it behind us.

"He has not returned," she said.

"You mean—?"

"I mean my husband."

"Frankly, I think it is almost as well that he should not have returned—at least, while I remain an inmate of your house. You can scarcely expect me to pass over his extraordinary behaviour in silence."

She stood staring at me in that strained, eager manner which I had noticed overnight. Her hands were clasped in front of her, her fingers were twisting and untwisting themselves in what seemed pure nervousness.

"I have been married to Mr. Barnes twelve months." As she paused, I nodded—I did not know what else to do. "I have regretted it ever since. There is a mystery about him."

"I am bound to admit that there is a good deal about him which is mysterious to me; but whether it is equally mysterious to you is another question."

"He is a mystery to me—he always has been." She paused again. She drew in her lips as if to moisten them. "You are a stranger to me, but I want a confidant. I must speak to some one."

"I beg that you will not make a confidant of me—I do assure you—"

As she interrupted me, her voice rose almost to a scream.

"I must speak to you—I will! I can endure no longer. Sit down and let me speak to you."

Perceiving that, unless I made a scene, I should have to let her at least say something, I did as she requested and sat down. I wished that she would sit down also, instead of standing in front of the door, twisting her hands and her body, and pulling faces—for only so can I describe what seemed to be the nervous spasms which were continually causing her to distort her attenuated countenance.

"I never wished to marry him," she began. "He made me."

"I suppose you mean that he made you in the sense in which all ladies, when their time comes, are made to marry."

"No, I don't. I never wanted to marry him—never. He was almost as great a stranger to me as you are. Why should I marry a perfect stranger, without a penny to his name—me, who had been a single woman, and content to be a single woman, for nearly forty years?"—I could not tell her; I am sure I had no notion.—"This house belongs to me; It was my mother's house before me. He came in one day and asked me if I wanted a waiter—came in with hardly a shoe to his foot. It was like his impudence! I did not want a waiter, and I told him so; but he mesmerised me, and made me have him!"

"Mesmerised you, Mrs. Barnes! You are joking!"

"I'm not joking." To do her justice any one who looked less like joking I never saw. "I've always been a nervous sort of a body. Directly he saw me he could do anything he liked with me. He was always mesmerising me. In less than a month he had mesmerised me into marrying him. As soon as we were married I began to think that he was mad!"—In that case, I told myself, that most promising couple must have been something very like a pair!—"He was always asking me if I would like to sell myself to the devil. He used to say that he would arrange it for me if I wanted. Then he used to dream out loud—such dreams! Night after night I've lain and listened to him, frightened half out of my wits. Then he took to walking in his sleep. The only thing he brought into the place was a little wooden box, tied up in a pocket-handkerchief. I never could make out what was in this box. Once when I asked him I thought he would have killed me. One night, in the middle of a dream, he got out of bed and went downstairs. Although I was so frightened that my knees were knocking together, I went after him. He came in here. This box of his was in that bureau—it's in that bureau now." She pointed to a tall, old-fashioned bureau which was just behind my chair. "He kept muttering to himself all the time; I could not catch all that he said, he spoke so low, but he repeated over and over again something about the devil. He took this box of his out of the bureau. He did something to it with his hands. What he did I don't know. I suppose there was a secret spring about it, or something. But though I've tried to make it out over and over again since then, I've never been able to find the secret of it to this day. When he handled it the top flew open. He put the box down upon that table; and I stood watching him in the open doorway—just about where I am standing now—without his having the least notion I was there. I believe that, if he had known, he would have killed me."

"Do you mean to say, while he was doing all you have described, that he was asleep?"

"Fast asleep."

"You are quite sure, Mrs. Barnes, that you also were not fast asleep?"

"Not me; I almost wish I had been. I've never had a good night's sleep from that hour to this. I've grown that thin, for want of it, that I'm nothing but a skeleton. As I was saying, when he had opened it he put the box down on the table. He gave a laugh which made my blood run cold."—She struck me as being the sort of woman whose blood on very slight provocation would run cold.—"Then he took something out of the box. When I saw what it was I thought I should have fainted." A nervous paroxysm seemed to pass all over her; her voice dropped to a whisper: "It was a woman's finger!"

"A woman's finger, Mrs. Barnes?"

"It was a woman's finger. There was a wedding-ring on it: it was too small for the finger, so that the ring seemed to have eaten into the flesh. He stood staring at this wedding-ring."

"What! staring! and he was fast asleep!"

"I don't know much about sleep-walkers; he was the first I ever saw, and I hope he'll be the last. But I do know that when he was sleep-walking his eyes were wide open, and he used to stare at things which, I suppose, he wanted to see, in a way which was horrible to look at. It was like that he stared at this wedding-ring. Then he said, right out loud: 'I'll cut you off one of these fine days, and see how you look upon my finger.' Then he put the finger down on the table, and out of the box he took three other fingers and a thumb."

"You are quite sure they were real, genuine, human fingers, Mrs. Barnes?"

"I know fingers when I see them, I suppose. You hear me out. He placed them on the table, nails uppermost, close together, just as the fingers are upon your own hand. He spoke to them. 'You'll never play any more of your devil's tricks with me that's a certainty!' he said. And he leered and grinned and chuckled more like a demon than a man. Then he took something out of the box, wrapped in a piece of calico. I saw that on the calico there were stains of blood. Out of it he took the palm of a woman's hand. Raising it to his lips, he kissed it, looking like the perfect devil that he was. He put it down palm downwards on the table, and he did something to the fingers. Then"— Mrs. Barnes gave utterance to a gasping sound, which it did not do one good to hear—"he picked it up, and I saw that by some devil's trickery he had joined the separate parts together, and made it look as if it were a perfect hand."

She stopped. I do not mind owning that if I had had my way, she would have stopped for good. Unfortunately I did not see my way to compel her to leave her tale unfinished.

"I suppose that at that dreadful sight I must have fainted, because the next thing I can remember is finding myself lying on the floor and the room all dark. For some time I dared scarcely breathe, far less move; I did not know where my husband might be. How I summoned up courage to enable me to creep upstairs, to this hour I do not know. When I did I found my husband fast asleep in bed."

"You really must excuse my asking, Mrs. Barnes, but do you happen to recollect what you ate for supper that night, and are you in the habit of suffering from nightmare?"

"Nightmare! That was the first time I watched him. I have watched him over and over again since then. I soon found out that regularly every Friday night he walked in his sleep, and went downstairs, and gloated over that dreadful hand."

14

"You say that he did this every Friday. Are you suggesting that with him Friday was some sort of anniversary?"

"I don't know. What was I to think? What was any one to think? Don't laugh at me—don't! You think I am a fool, or lying. You shall see the hand for yourself, and tell me what you make of it. I will show it you, if I have to break his box open with a hammer."

In a state of considerable and evident excitement, she crossed the room. I rose to enable her to approach the bureau. She took a small canvas bag out of the pocket of her dress. Out of this bag she took some keys.

"He has my keys. He made me give him them. He never knew that I had duplicates. But I always have had. He seldom went outside the front door; I think he was afraid of being seen in the streets. Whenever he did go I used to lock myself in here, and try to find the spring which opened the box. I had an idea that there might be something in it which I had not seen. I will open it now, if I have to smash it into splinters."

She let down the flap of the bureau. Within there were nests of drawers, and one small centre cupboard. This cupboard she unlocked. When she had done so, she gave a stifled exclamation. "It has gone!" she said.

I stooped beside her. "What has gone?"

She turned to me a face which was ghastly in its revelation of abject terror. Her voice had suddenly degenerated into a sort of panting hiss.

"The box! It was here last night. After he had gone I unlocked the bureau, and I looked, and saw it was there." She caught me by the arm, she gripped me with a strength of which, in her normal condition, I should imagine her incapable. "He must have come back like a thief in the night and taken it. He may be hidden somewhere in the house this moment. Oh, my God!"

CHAPTER III

THE MAN IN THE DOORWAY

I called at Messrs. Cleaver and Caxton's to ask what I should do with the four five-pound notes which had arrived in the letter. The individual who had taken me to the hotel was the only person in the office. It seemed, from his own statement, that he was Mr. Cleaver, the senior partner. When he learned why I had come, he laughed.

"Do with them? Why, spend them, or throw them into the river, or give them to me."

I hesitated. The truth is, the situation threatened to become too complicated. I had an uneasy consciousness that the something which James Southam was to hear of might be something to his exceeding disadvantage. I had heard enough of that sort of thing of late. I did not wish to stand in somebody else's shoes for the sake of hearing more. I resolved to have some sort of understanding with Mr. Cleaver.

"Who is Duncan Rothwell? Is he the client for whom you are acting?"

Mr. Cleaver was occupying himself in tearing a piece of paper into tiny shreds with his fingers. He replied to my question with another. "Why do you ask?"

"Because the signature attached to the letter which brought the bank-notes is Duncan Rothwell; and, as to my knowledge, I know no Duncan Rothwell, I should like to know who Duncan Rothwell is."

"Do you mind my looking at the letter?"

I did not mind. I let him look at it. He read it through.

"If you will take a hint from me, Mr. Southam, I think I should advise you to restrain your not unnatural curiosity, and wait for things to take their course."

"But, unless I am careful, I may find myself in a false position. I may not be the required James Southam. In fact, I don't mind telling you that I don't believe I am. I am acquainted with no Duncan Rothwell. His whole letter is double Dutch to me. There may be dozens of James Southams about."

"Recent inhabitants of Dulborough? I thought Dulborough was a mere hamlet."

"So it is."

"How long did you live there?"

"I was born and bred in the place."

"Have you any relatives of your own name?"

"I have not a relative in the world."

"If, as you say, you were born and bred in such a place as Dulborough, I presume that you had some knowledge of the inhabitants?'

"I believe I knew something of every creature in all the country side."

"And did you know anything of another James Southam?"

"That is the queer part of it. So far as I know, I was the only Southam thereabouts."

Mr. Cleaver laughed.

"According to your own statement, it appears that, to put it mildly, there is at least a possibility of your being the James Southam we have been instructed to find. Frankly, Mr. Southam, we know very little more about the matter than you do yourself. We have simply been instructed to discover the present address of James Southam, at one time of Dulborough, and we have done so."

"Is that the case?"

From their manner the day before I had suspected that Messrs. Cleaver and Caxton might be merely, as it were, lay figures, and that it was somebody else who held the strings.

"There is something else I should like to mention: I wish to change my hotel." Mr. Cleaver stared.

"Change your hotel? Why? Isn't it good enough?"

"It is not that exactly. It is the domestic arrangements which are not to my taste."

"The domestic arrangements? What do you mean?"

I did not know how to explain; or rather, I did not know how much to explain.

"What do you know of Mrs. Barnes's husband?"

"Really, Mr. Southam, your bump of curiosity appears to be fully developed. What has Mrs. Barnes's husband to do with you—or with me? If you don't like your present quarters you are at perfect liberty to change them; —only in that case you must become responsible for your own expenditure." I turned to go. "One moment. If you intend to change your quarters, perhaps, under the circumstances, you will be so good as to let us know where you propose to go."

"I will let you know if I do go. At any rate, until to-morrow I intend to remain where I am."

Whether it would have been better for me, considering the tragedy which followed, never to have returned to Mrs. Barnes's house at all, is more than I can say. That particular tragedy might not have happened, but, looking at the matter from a purely personal and selfish point of view, whether that would have been better for me, or worse, is another question altogether.

That night I went to a music-hall, changing one of Mr. Rothwell's notes to enable me to do so. Afterwards I supped at a restaurant in the Strand. Then I returned to the hotel to bed. I was more than half afraid of being waylaid by Mrs. Barnes. But, to my relief, it was the maidservant who let me in. I saw and heard nothing of the landlady. I spent the night in peace.

A telegram was brought me the next morning after breakfast. It was short and to the point—

"Shall be with you at twelve-thirty.—DUNCAN ROTHWELL."

As I perceived that it had been despatched from Derby station, I concluded that Mr. Rothwell had telegraphed while in the very act of journeying to town. Half-past twelve arrived, and no one, and nothing came for me. About a quarter to one I went into the hall with some vague idea of seeing if some likely looking person might be coming down the street. The hall was really nothing but a narrow passage. The front door was open. With his feet just inside the open doorway was a man lying face downwards on the floor. My first impulse was to beat a retreat, because I at once jumped to the conclusion that Mr. Barnes, or Mr. James Southam, or whatever the landlady's mysterious husband's name might be, had returned to the bosom of his family, not only unpleasantly inclined, but drunk. A brief inspection from the other end of the passage, however, made it sufficiently clear that, whoever the recumbent individual was, it was not the gentleman who had first waited on and then assaulted me.

I could see that he was, in every way, a larger man. His silk hat had fallen sufficiently off his head to enable one to perceive that he was bald. As I stood and watched him, I began to be conscious of a curiously unpleasant feeling. He lay so still; and in such an uncomfortable posture. He was a big, fat man;

it struck me that he must weigh some seventeen or eighteen stone. He had fallen flat upon his stomach; his face was so close to the floor that he must have found it difficult to breathe. His right arm was bent under him, in a way which disagreeably suggested a broken limb. The man must surely be something more than drunk. He must, I told myself, have fallen in a fit.

With an indefinable feeling of repugnance, I advanced to give him aid. I bent over him. I laid my hand upon his shoulder; I withdrew it with a start. The man's coat was wet. I glanced at my own palm; it was covered with some red pigment. Thoroughly aroused I sprang to my feet.

"Help! Mrs. Barnes!" I cried.

Mrs. Barnes and the maidservant came running up together.

"Mrs. Barnes," I said, still staring at the patch of red upon my hand, "I believe there has been murder done."

"Murder! Oh, my God! Do you think he did it?"

I looked at her. I knew what she meant, but I did not answer her, "You had better send for the police, and for a medical man."

It was the servant who retained sufficient presence of mind to catch at my suggestion.

"Doctor Granger lives across the road. I'll fetch him!"

She did fetch him. Luckily the doctor was at home. So soon as he learned what urgent need there was for his services, he came hurrying to render them. Presently a policeman came upon the scene. He was followed by others. They kept the street clear, for some distance from the hotel, of the crowd which began rapidly to gather. The whole house, as it were, was taken in charge.

CHAPTER IV

THE ALIAS

"This man was alive within the last few minutes." That was the doctor's verdict. "He is still quite warm." The doctor looked at me. "What do you know about the matter?"

"Nothing. I was expecting a visitor. As he was late, I came down from the coffee-room, and went into the hall with the intention of seeing if he was coming. As I was coming down the stairs I saw this man lying on the floor."

The body had been moved into the little front room on the ground floor, which, I afterwards learned, was used as a private sitting-room for such visitors to the house as chose to pay for one. There were present in the room, besides myself, the doctor, a young man with a shrewd but kindly face, an inspector of police, a sergeant, who kept the door, while Mrs. Barnes and the maid kept each other close company in the corner by the fireplace. When I had answered the doctor, the inspector questioned me upon his own account.

"What is that upon your hand?"

I held out the hand to which he referred.

"Blood! This unfortunate man's blood! When I saw him lying on the floor my impression was that he was either drunk or in a fit. I laid my hand upon his shoulder with a view of rousing him. Directly I did so I found that his coat was wet. When I withdrew my hand I saw that it was covered with blood. It was then I realised that there had been foul play."

The dead man had been laid on the table. It was not large enough to hold the whole of him, so that his feet hung over the edge. He was a big man all over—in particular, he had one of the biggest heads I ever saw. There was not a hair on the top. But on his large, fat cheeks were what used to be called mutton-chop whiskers, which were in colour a dirty red. He was dressed from top to toe in glossy black broadcloth. He wore black kid gloves upon his hands. In the centre of his wide expanse of shirtfront was, so far as I was a judge of such things, a large diamond stud. A heavy gold chain spanned his waistcoat.

"Is this the person you were expecting?" inquired the inspector.

"That is more than I can tell you. The person I was expecting was to me personally a stranger."

"What was his name?"

"Duncan Rothwell. I received a telegram from him this morning to say that he would be here by half-past twelve. Here is the telegram."

I handed it to the inspector.

"Half-past twelve. And when do you say that you discovered this man on the floor?"

"About a quarter to one. When I gave the alarm the landlady of the hotel and the servant came running to me immediately. They will be able to tell you what time it was; and I should say that the doctor was here within five minutes."

The inspector turned to the doctor.

"And what was the time, sir, when you arrived?"

"I should say as nearly as possible about ten minutes to one. I lunch at one; I was just going to wash when I was called."

"And how long do you say, sir, he had then been dead?"

"He had probably been alive five minutes before."

"Then, in that case, he must have been alive when this man says he entered the hall." The inspector pointed to me.

"I do not say that. The man was stabbed in the back, under the left shoulder, probably just as he was in the act of entering the house. I have only made a superficial examination, but I think it probable that the blow killed him in an instant—before, that is, he could breathe the breath which he was breathing, as it were, right out. And I do say this, that if this gentleman had entered the hall a minute before he actually did, he would have seen the man in the very act of being murdered."

The inspector turned again to me.

"Where did this Mr. Duncan Rothwell live?"

"That also is more than I can tell you. The fact is, I know nothing whatever about him. A firm of solicitors placed him in communication with me."

"What was he coming to see you about?"

"With reference to this advertisement."

I gave the inspector the advertisement which had placed me in the position which, so far, did not promise to be much to my advantage.

"What is your name?"

"James Southam."

"Are you the James Southam here alluded to?"

"That, again, is more than I can tell you. I saw that advertisement the day before yesterday. I at once communicated with Messrs. Cleaver and Caxton. Yesterday I received this letter, and this morning the telegram which you already have."

The inspector carefully read the letter which had come to me signed "Duncan Rothwell." Then, without asking with your leave or by your leave, he placed the letter, the advertisement, and the telegram in his pocket-book, and the pocket-book in his pocket. The action struck me as extremely, and indeed unpleasantly, significant.

An examination of the dead man's pockets disclosed the somewhat curious fact that they contained nothing but a massive gold watch, without a maker's name; a sheaf of bank-notes, which, unenclosed in any cover, was simply thrust in the breast-pocket of his coat, and consisted of no less than one hundred ten-pound notes; some gold and silver coins—four pounds, thirteen shillings, if I remember rightly—in a plain leather purse; and, in an apparently forgotten corner of his right-hand waistcoat pocket, was a torn scrap of a visiting card. On it was the name, "Raymond." But the card was torn in such a manner that, whether this was a surname or a Christian name, there was, as the police would themselves have said, no evidence to show. But beyond these articles there was absolutely nothing which would serve or could be used as a means of identification. It almost seemed as if the dead man had taken care that there should be nothing about him by means of which he could be identified.

As soon as the inspector seemed disposed to allow me to quit his presence I went straight away to Messrs. Cleaver and Caxton. Again I found the senior partner alone. My appearance seemed to surprise him; possibly in my bearing there was something which was a trifle suggestive of the condition of my mind.

"Well, has Mr. Rothwell been?"

I shut the door behind me, looking him full in the face.

"You appear to have let me in for a nice little thing, Mr. Cleaver."

"What do you mean?"

"It is what you mean I intend to understand before I leave this room. You will be so good as to answer me one or two questions, Mr. Cleaver. First, is

22

Mr. Duncan Rothwell the name of the client for whom you have been acting?"

He leaned back in his chair, regarding me with rather a curious smile.

"You have a singular method of address, Mr. Southam. Before I answer this question perhaps you will answer mine. Has Mr. Rothwell been to see you?"

"What does he look like?"

"Look like!" Again the curious smile. "You continue to answer question with question. Tell me, sir, has any one calling himself Duncan Rothwell been to see you? We will discuss the question of what he looked like afterwards."

I paused before I spoke again, then keenly noted the effect of my words.

"For all I know, Mr. Duncan Rothwell lies murdered at Mrs. Barnes's hotel."

Mr. Cleaver sprang to his feet. "Murdered!"

"Precisely! Some one lies there murdered. If you will tell me what he looks like I will tell you if it is Mr. Duncan Rothwell."

Not unnaturally, Mr. Cleaver appeared bewildered.

"Explain yourself a little more clearly, Mr. Southam; and, to begin with, will you be so good as to answer Yes or No to my question. Has any one calling himself Duncan Rothwell been to see you?"

I told him what had happened—so far as I understood it. His amazement unmistakably was genuine.

"You say that the dead man had nothing on him by means of which he could be recognised. Then, in that case, we can do nothing to assist in his identification; we ourselves have never seen Mr. Duncan Rothwell in our lives. All our communications with him have been by letter."

He acknowledged one thing: that the person for whom they had been acting was Mr. Duncan Rothwell. But, beyond that one fact, I learned nothing at all. He protested that Mr. Duncan Rothwell had instructed them, by letter, to advertise for a James Southam, of Dulborough, and that that was all they knew of the matter. He even suggested that, since I was James Southam, I, if I chose, could fill up the blanks.

When I returned to the hotel, little wiser than I left it, as soon as I set foot inside the door the inspector of police, clapping his hand upon my shoulder, drew me aside. I did not like the fashion in which he addressed me at all.

"See here, Mr. Southam. I do not wish to make myself disagreeable, but I need scarcely point out to you that there are circumstances in this case which are, to say the least of it, peculiar. I may as well tell you that your movements will be under the surveillance of the police; and, should you make any attempt to elude us we may consider it our duty to place you in safe custody."

"That's all right," I replied. "Lock me up and hang me, do! It only needs some little trifle of that kind to make the situation altogether what it should be. The man is a perfect stranger to me, and I know no more how he came to his death than the man in the moon; which things are, possibly, a sufficient reason why the police should make of me one of their proverbial examples."

It struck me that the inspector did not altogether know what to make of me; Although he did not arrest me, to all intents and purposes he might almost as well have done. Until the inquest took place the hotel was practically in charge, with everybody in it. A policeman slept on the premises; other policemen were continually about the premises, asking questions and making themselves objectionable both by day and night. I myself began to feel that I had a haunted, hangdog sort of air. As for Mrs. Barnes, if she had not a great crime upon her conscience, it was not because she did not look it. She seemed to be growing hourly thinner. I knew very well that she was full of a great anxiety to say a word or two to me in private, but dared not for fear of prying eyes and ears. She solved the difficulty in her own way by pinning a note to my pillow, so that I found it on going to bed on the night before the inquest.

It had neither beginning nor end, and ran something like this; every word was underlined—

"Say nothing to-morrow about my husband, for God's sake! I am quite sure that he had nothing to do with this deed of horror—you know that he had not—and I know! No good purpose will be served by dragging him into it, and so bringing on me greater ruin than has come already!"

As I read this scarcely judicious appeal I told myself that Mrs. Barnes was certainly wrong in saying that I knew that her mysterious husband had had nothing to do with the crime which had been wrought. As a matter of fact, I knew nothing.

The more I reflected, however, the less I liked the look of the circumstances, which seemed to suggest a guilty knowledge on the part of my whilom friend, the waiter. It appeared at least possible that he was the James Southam who had been actually advertised for, and that he was very well aware that Duncan Rothwell had something to say to him which was, very distinctly, not to his advantage. Looking at the violence which, without hesitation, he had used towards me, was it not conceivable that he might have, and indeed had, used still greater violence towards Mr. Rothwell?

The inquest was not over in a day, though the only light it threw upon the crime went to prove the identity of the murdered man. A singular state of things the evidence upon this point revealed—by no means tending to elucidate the mystery. The dead man actually turned out to be Jonas Hartopp —the head, and, in fact, the sole remaining partner, in the well-known firm of manufacturing jewellers—Hartopp and Company. The strange part of the business was that he seemed to have been Duncan Rothwell as well—that is, he had assumed that name for reasons which were very far from being plain.

Hartopp and Company were a Birmingham firm—a wealthy one. Jonas Hartopp himself had had the reputation of being as rich as a reasonable man would care to be. Duncan Rothwell had written to Messrs. Cleaver and Caxton from Liverpool, where he had taken rooms, as it would seem, for the special purpose of communicating with them.

He had never occupied the rooms, but had given the most peremptory instructions that all letters and telegrams should at once be forwarded to an address at Aston. The address at Aston turned out to be a tobacconist's shop. The tobacconist at once recognised the dead man as being the person he had known as Duncan Rothwell. Why the wealthy Birmingham jeweller, Jonas Hartopp, had chosen to masquerade as Duncan Rothwell, or what was the something to his advantage which he proposed to communicate to James Southam, there was not a shred or tittle of evidence to show; nor was there a thread of light thrown upon the shadows which enveloped the mystery of his sudden death.

As it chanced, no question was asked me while I was in the witness-box which gave me an opportunity of bringing in the incident of Mrs. Barnes's husband. I had a sufficiently bad time of it without being actuated by a burning desire to involve myself in further complications. Never in my life had I been so badgered. They would not accept my plain statement that I had not the faintest notion why James Southam had been advertised for, or who had advertised for him, or what was the something which he was to learn to his advantage. The coroner and the police, and, for the matter of that, the public too, appeared to be under the impression that, since I owned that my name was James Southam, therefore I held the key of the mystery in the hollow of my hand; or, at any rate, that I ought to. They had raked up the circumstances of my life from my earliest days; they had made all sorts of inquiries about me in all sorts of directions, yet they could find nothing which could fairly be said to tell against me; and that for the sufficient, and, from my point of view, satisfactory reason, that there was nothing to find.

Notwithstanding which, when the inquiry closed, I was conscious that more than one person in court, and a good many out of it, cherished the impression that I had had a hand indirectly, if not directly, in the murdered man's despatch, the verdict of the coroner's jury being that Jonas Hartopp, otherwise known as Duncan Rothwell, had been murdered by some person or persons unknown.

CHAPTER V

THE NEW GUEST.

Oddly enough it was not until I was smarting under the feelings occasioned by the reflection that I had come out of the inquiry with a smirch upon my character that it occurred to me what a fool I had been, when I was in the witness-box, in not going even out of my way to transfer suspicion from myself to the scamp whom Mrs. Barnes had assured me was her husband. I arrived, then and there, at a resolution. I would play, on lines of my own, that favourite part in fiction—the role of the amateur detective. I would trace to their sources the various threads which had become complicated in such a tangled web of crime. I would unravel them, one by one. Single-handed, if necessary, I would make the whole thing plain.

In theory, an excellent resolution; situated as I was, not an easy one to put into practice. Before the end of the coroner's inquest Messrs. Cleaver and Caxton informed me that their guarantee to provide for the expenses of my sojourn at Mrs. Barnes's establishment thenceforward was withdrawn. Of the four banknotes which had come to me in Duncan Rothwell's letter about fifteen pounds remained. If that sum might be credited to my account, on the debit side of the column was the injury which my connection with the affair had, at least temporarily, done my character. If before I had found it difficult to obtain remunerative employment, I should find it now still harder.

On the morning after the close of the inquiry I was meditating taking an immediate departure from the house in which I had met with experiences which had been to anything but my advantage, when Mrs. Barnes came into the room. Her worries had worn her almost to a shadow. I felt that, if she continued to diminish at the same rate long, she soon, literally, would entirely waste away. Her nervous tricks seemed to have become accentuated. She stood rubbing her hands together, apparently for the moment at a loss for something to say.

"I hope, sir, that you are not going?"

"Then you hope wrong, Mrs. Barnes. I certainly am going, and that at once."

"You mustn't sir—you really mustn't."

"You are wrong again, Mrs. Barnes, for I really must, if on one account only—that I am not in a position to pay your terms."

She gave a sudden movement forward, coming to lean with both her hands upon the table. Her voice dropped to that odd, palpitating whisper of which she seemed to be so fond.

"You needn't let that trouble you. You can live board and lodging free, and you'll be welcome."

I observed her closely. In her face there was something which was positively uncanny. If ever a person had a haunted look it was Mrs. Barnes.

"Why do you make to me such a proposition? Do you consider that I am the sort of person who would be willing to snatch at anybody's charity, or are you in the habit of giving strangers board and lodging free?"

"Indeed, no; but it's different with you. If you leave me now I shall not dare to stay in the house, and that's the truth. I feel as if you were guarding me; as if hungry eyes were on the house, seeking for a chance to work me evil, but that the hidden watchers dare not come in to do that to me which they desire while my roof still shelters you. Sir, do you think that 'he' did it?"

"Do I think that who did what?"

"Do you think that my husband killed that man?"

"To be frank with you, I think it extremely possible that he knows as much of the business as may altogether be good for him—more, for instance, than you or I. I have been reproaching myself for having done as you requested, and not having at least alluded to the gentleman in question when giving my evidence before the coroner."

My words set her trembling.

"You did quite right. You would have been sorry for it afterwards. I cannot tell you why or how, but I am certain that my husband had no more to do with that deed of blood than you or I."

The woman's intense earnestness made me stare.

"I can only say, Mrs. Barnes, that I regret that I am unable to share your certainty."

"That is one reason why I ask you—why I implore you to stay. There is a cloud hanging over you and over me—it is the same cloud! If you stay I feel that it may be lifted; but, if you leave, it may rest on us for ever."

What she said was nonsense pure and simple. Still, I suffered myself to be persuaded. I agreed to stay on—at any rate, for a time. The satisfaction with which she received my decision was so pronounced that one might have thought that I had done her the greatest service in the world.

I went out in the afternoon. When I came back in the evening, not a little to my surprise, my food was brought me by a man. I stared at him askance. Hitherto the whole service of the house, in which I had been the only guest, had been done by the maid. Now I found myself confronted by a quite irreproachable-looking waiter, attired in the orthodox costume of his kind. His presence was so unexpected that I found it impossible to conceal my astonishment.

"Who the deuce are you?" I blurted out.

The fellow began to smirk in reply. "New waiter, sir—only came this afternoon, sir!"

"I had no notion that Mrs. Barnes contemplated making such an addition to her establishment."

"No, sir; perhaps not, sir. Business is very slack just now, but the season is coming on, and the house will very soon be full."

This was emphatically a lie. So far from the season just coming on, in an hotel-keeper's sense, it was rapidly drawing to an end; and so far as Mrs. Barnes was personally concerned, apparently a bitter one, too. What she wanted, circumstanced as she was, with such a gorgeous individual as this about the place, or what she could find for him to do, surpassed my comprehension.

The fellow bustled about the room, pretending to busy himself, in accordance with a trick of his trade, with nothing at all.

"Been here long, sir?"

"You know very well how long I have been here."

"Beg pardon, sir, how's that?"

"You have read it in the papers. Don't feign ignorance with me, my man."

The fellow turned away. He was industriously polishing an already spotless glass.

"You allude to the recent unfortunate occurrence, sir? I believe that I did see something about it."

"You believe! Is that all? You are perfectly aware that you are as well up in what you call the recent occurrence as I am. You know all about me; how I came into the house, when I came, my name, and everything."

I do not know why I said this, but I did say it, and I felt that it was true.

The man seemed taken aback.

"Mrs. Barnes did mention your name," he murmured.

"You knew it without her mentioning it. You can leave the room. When I want you I will ring."

I was glad to be rid of him. His presence seemed to chafe me. I knew not why. He was not ill-looking. His bearing was wholly respectful; and yet some instinct had seemed to warn me that while I was in his near neighbourhood it would be just as well that I should be upon my guard.

When I had eaten I sallied forth in quest of Mrs. Barnes. Her nervous system had not improved since the morning; even the sight of me seemed to fill her with terror. Her eyes looked at everything except at me. I wondered if some disaster had been added to the sum of her already over-numerous troubles.

"You have a new waiter," I began.

"Yes." She spoke in a stammering whisper. Her features were agitated with the former reminiscence of St. Vitus's Dance. "Yes; a new waiter."

"I hope very sincerely, for your sake, Mrs. Barnes, that he may ere long have other guests to wait upon besides myself."

"Yes." The same irresolute muttering. "Yes; I hope he may."

"I had no idea that you thought of making an engagement of the kind just now."

"No—I don't think—I told you."

What was the matter with the woman? Why did she persist in speaking in that tone of voice, as if she was fearful of being overheard! And why did she apparently not dare to allow her eyes to rest, even for a moment, on my face? She had been so effusive in the morning. Now, on a sudden, she had returned to the condition of almost doddering terror which had marked her bearing during the time we had a policeman quartered in the house.

"Where did you get the man? What is his name? And what do you know of him?"

As I put my questions I thought for a moment that she was going to favour me with one of her frenzied bursts of confidence. But while I waited for her to speak, all at once her frame became rigid. I seemed to see the unspoken words lying on her lips. Turning to discover the cause of the obvious change in her manner, I found that the new waiter had opened the door and, unannounced, had entered the room. At sight of him her agitation again assumed the upper hand.

"I—I must ask you to excuse me, sir. I have something which I must do."

I did excuse her; but when I had left her I decided in my own mind that my instinct had been right, and that there was more in the new waiter than met the eye. It seemed scarcely likely that even a landlady of such an eccentric type as Mrs. Barnes would increase her staff when the only guest which her house contained was such an emphatically unprofitable one as I bade fair to be.

However, in one respect the position of affairs was destined to be speedily changed. The house received not only another guest, but also one who bade fair to be as profitable a one as a landlady's heart could wish. It was on the day immediately following that Mrs. Lascelles-Trevor arrived. I had been out all the morning and afternoon, renewing the weary search for employment which might provide me with the means for obtaining my daily bread. The first intimation I had of her arrival was when, having dined, I was thinking of a quiet pipe, and of an early retirement to bed.

CHAPTER VI

THE WOMAN WITH ONE HAND

"Mrs. Lascelles-Trevor's compliments, sir, and would you mind stepping upstairs?"

I had a lighted match in my hand, and was in the very act of applying it to the bowl of my pipe when the latest importation in waiters brought me the message.

"Mrs. Lascelles-Trevor?" I let the match go out. "And pray who may Mrs. Lascelles-Trevor be?"

"The lady who arrived to-day, sir, and who has taken a private sitting-room —No. 8."

"Indeed! And what does Mrs. Lascelles-Trevor want with me?"

"I don't know, sir; she asked me to give you her compliments, and would you be so kind as to step upstairs."

I stepped upstairs, wondering. I was received by a tall and somewhat ponderous woman, who was dressed in a dark-blue silk costume, almost as if she were going to a ball. She half rose from the couch as I came in, inclining her head in my direction with what struck me as a slightly patronising smile. She spoke in a loud, hearty tone of voice, which was marked by what struck me as being a Yorkshire twang.

"It is so good of you to come to see me, Mr. Southam. I was really more than half afraid to ask you. As it is, I beg ten thousand pardons, but I do so want you to write me a letter."

"To write you a letter? I am afraid I am a little slow of comprehension."

"I have lost my hand." She stretched out her right arm. Both arms were bare to the shoulder. I could not but notice how beautifully they were moulded, their massive contours, their snowy whiteness. She wore gloves which reached nearly to her elbows. So far as I could judge there appeared to be a hand inside of both. She seemed to read my thoughts, still continuing to hold her right arm out in front of her.

"You think my hand is gloved? I always wear it so. But the glove conceals a dummy. Come and feel it." I bowed. I was content to take her at her word; I

32

had no wish to put her to the actual test. "I have never been able to gain complete control over my left hand—to use it as if it were my right. I suppose it is because I am not clever enough. I can scribble with it, but only scribble. When I desire to have a letter properly written I am dependent upon outsiders' help. Will you write one for me now?"

It was an odd request for a new-comer at an hotel to address to a perfect stranger, but I complied. The letter she dictated, and which I wrote at her dictation, seemed to me the merest triviality—a scribble would have served the purpose just as well. She chattered all the time that I was writing, and, when I had finished, she went on chattering still. All at once she broke into a theme to which I ought to have become accustomed, but had not.

"Do you know, Mr. Southam, that I have been reading about this dreadful murder case? How the papers have all been full of it! And I don't mind telling you, as a matter of fact, that in a sort of a way it was that which has brought me to this hotel."

If that were so, I retorted, then her tastes were individual; she perceived attractions where the average man saw none. She laughed.

"I don't know that it was exactly that, but the truth is, Mr. Southam, I was interested in you." The way in which she emphasised the pronoun a little startled me. "I made up my mind that I would ferret you out directly I got to the hotel, and that then, if I liked the look of you, would make you an offer. You see how frank I am."

She certainly was frank to a fault, in one sense. And yet I wondered. As I replied to her my tone was grim.

"It is very good of you. And now that, as I take it for granted that you do like the look of me—as you can scarcely fail to do—may I inquire what is the nature of the offer you propose to make?"

She laughed again. Possibly my perceptions were unusually keen, but, all the time, it occurred to me that there was about her a something—an atmosphere, if you will—which was not exactly suggestive of laughter. Unless I was mistaken, her faculties were as much on the alert as mine were. She was engaged in summing me up when she feigned to be least observant.

"You must understand, Mr. Southam, that I know all about you which the papers had to tell, and that was not a little! So we are not exactly strangers. At least, that is, you are not wholly a stranger to me. Besides which, I myself once knew a person whose name was Southam."

I started. The woman's eyes were fixed on me, although she pretended to be trifling with her dress.

"You knew a person whose name was Southam. Indeed! Who was it, a man or a woman?"

She ignored my question.

"Have you any relatives of your own name?

"Not that I am aware of, though there seems to be more than one Southam about in the world. What Southam was it you knew?"

Her tone was ostentatiously indifferent. "Oh, it doesn't matter. It was a long time ago, and, as you say, I suppose there are heaps of Southams about in the world. I only wanted to explain to you that you were not so absolutely unknown to me as the fact that this is our first actual meeting might lead you to imagine. Will you allow me to ask if you are still seeking employment? I thought, from what I read in the papers, that it was just possible you might be."

"You   have   supposed   correctly.   I   am."

"Would you like to fill the post of secretary?"

"Of secretary?" I paused for a moment to consider—not the suggestion of such a post, but the source from whence the suggestion came. "To whom?"

"To me."

"It is very kind of you, but do you clearly understand, madam, that you are speaking to a person whose character is under a cloud?"

"Because you were suspected of having murdered that man?"

Her question was brutal in its candour.

"Precisely. Because I was suspected, and, for all I know, still am."

"The people who suspected you were fools. I will back my capacity as a judge of character, even at sight, against their suspicions. You are not of the stuff of which murderers are made."

Her tone was short and sharp—I had almost written sarcastic—as if she thought it a shame to a man not to be made of the stuff of which murderers are. She went on, speaking quickly, even brusquely.

"I will trust you, if you, on your part, will trust me. As I have told you, and as I will prove to you, if—as I almost believe—you doubt me, I have lost my hand. See!" Hastily, before I could stop her, she began to unbutton her right glove. She only unloosed a button or two, when the whole thing, glove, hand and all, came clean away, and she held out towards me her handless arm. I stared, at a loss for words, not a little shocked—the disfigurement was so dreadful, and seemed to have been so recent. Her voice grew bitter. "I lost that hand under circumstances which impressed its loss upon my memory. As it were, I seem to be losing it anew, every hour of every day. It has left me impotent. Will you relieve my impotence? Will you become my secretary? There will not be much for you to do, but there will be something; the salary which I shall pay you will not be a large one, but it will, perhaps, suffice till something better offers; I will give you a hundred pounds a year, and, as they say in the advertisements, all found. Do not give me your answer at once. It may be that I shall stay in the hotel some time, and, at any rate, while I am here, possibly you will not refuse to act as my amanuensis. You can see with your own eyes how much I am in want of one."

Again she drew my attention to her mangled arm. As she suggested, I neither accepted nor declined her offer there and then; it was one which needed consideration from more points than one. For instance, while she did know something of me—if what she had read in the newspaper reports could be called knowledge—I knew literally nothing of her; for all I could tell, she might be an adventuress lately freed from the purlieus of a gaol. I did consent to do any secretarial work she might require during her stay in the hotel. By the time she left it I might be able to see my way more clearly than I did just then.

I saw a good deal of Mrs. Lascelles-Trevor during the few days which followed, and the more I saw of her the less I could make her out. There was a good deal of work for me to do, such as it was. I wondered if she had brought it with her in order to furnish her with an excuse to give me occupation. There were papers for me to copy—papers which seemed to be of the very slightest importance. While I was supposed to be engaged in copying them, she interrupted me without remorse, and talked and talked and talked. During those conversations she learned a great deal of my history, while I ascertained nothing at all of hers. I found that she was a woman of quick and imperious temper: to fence with one of her interminable questions annoyed her; to have declined point-blank to answer one would have involved an immediate breach. If I took service with her, it would be with my eyes open; I should have to be prepared for squalls. Though she gave me employment as if she were bestowing charity, she would expect and require perfect obedience from me in return.

I do not think that, as a rule, I am quick in taking dislike at a person, but there did, in spite of myself, grow up in my mind a sense of antipathy towards Mrs. Lascelles-Trevor. I felt as if she were watching me; pumping me, turning me inside out, as if I were some old glove; playing with me with that cruel sort of enjoyment with which a cat plays with a mouse, and I did not find the feeling an agreeable one.

To add to my comfort, I had an uneasy consciousness that the new waiter had an attentive eye upon my movements in a non-waiterial sense. It was an eye for which I did not thank him; I almost suspected that he was playing the part of a sleepless spy. I half believed that, not infrequently, he was an unseen auditor of my interviews with Mrs. Lascelles-Trevor—I should like to have caught him in the act! One night I could not sleep, I found that I had left my pipe downstairs. I started off to get it; I had scarcely got outside the bedroom door when I all but stumbled over the new waiter. Before I had discovered who it was, I had pinned him to the floor. He was profuse in his apologies, but I do not think that he could altogether have liked the way in which I handled him.

CHAPTER VII

THE SECOND ENCOUNTER

I began, as the days went by, to be more and more a prey to unhealthy, and apparently unreasonable doubts and fears—fears which, in truth, were so intangible that they were without form and void, but which were very real for all that. I began to feel as if a net were being drawn tighter and tighter round me, and as if every step I took was beset by hidden dangers. Such a mental condition was as I have said, an unhealthy one. I realised that well enough, and I had been wandering one evening to and fro on the Embankment, striving to free myself, if only for a time, from the imaginary mists and shadows which seemed to compass me about, when as I was turning into the street in which stood Mrs. Barnes's hotel, I saw a man crouching in the darkness of the wall. What was the man's purpose I had no doubt: he was seeking for concealment. He had seen me before I saw him, and was endeavouring to escape my scrutiny.

I took him to be the new waiter. I supposed that I had caught him in the act of spying on me at last. I turned swiftly on him, and before he could retreat I had him by the shoulders.

"Before I let you go, my friend, you will be so good as to tell me, now and here, what is the cause of the extreme interest which you evidently take in my proceedings."

That was what I said to him; but already, before I had said my say right out, I perceived that I was wrong: that the man I had hold of was not the man I thought he was. This man was shorter and of slighter build, and he showed more signs of fight than, within my experience, the other had evinced. He wriggled in my grasp like an eel, but, holding tightly on to him, I dragged him a little into the light.

When I succeeded in getting a glimpse at him there came from between my lips a series of interjections:—

"You!—James Southam!—Mr. Barnes! Good God!"

I had hardly spoken when he knocked me down. I was so taken by surprise that I was unable to offer the least resistance; he felled me again, as he had felled me before, as if I had been a ninepin. By the time I had realised what had happened I was lying on my back on the pavement. His hand was on my throat, and his knee was on my chest. He was peering closely into my face—so closely that I could feel his breath upon my cheeks.

"It's you again, is it? I thought it was. Don't you make a noise, or I'll choke the life right out of you. You tell me, straight out, what it is you want with me—do you hear?"

As if to drive his question well home, he gave my head a sharp tap against the pavement. His strength must have been prodigious. I was conscious that, with him above me thus and with that iron grasp upon my throat, I was wholly at his mercy. The hour was late. Although almost within a stone's throw of the Strand, the place was solitary; not a creature might pass just where we were the whole night through.

"Take your hand from my windpipe—I cannot speak—you are choking me," I gasped.

"Give me your word you will make no noise if I do. See here!"

He was clutching a knife—as ugly a looking knife as ever I saw. He brandished it before my eyes.

"I give my word," I managed to utter.

He relaxed his hold. It was a comfort to be again able to freely inflate my lungs, though the continued presence of his knee on my chest was none too pleasant. With the point of his knife he actually pricked my nose.

"Don't you try to move, or I will cut your throat as if you were a pig. Lie still and answer my questions—and straight, mind, or you'll be sorry. What is it you want with me?"

"I want nothing from you—I have never wanted anything. You have been under an entire misapprehension throughout."

Once more, with gruesome sportiveness, he tickled my nose with his knife.

"Stow that, my lad! It's no good trying to catch this bird with salt. How did you come to know that my name was James Southam?"

"I never did know it. The simple truth is that that name happened to be mine."

"What's that?"

"I say that that name happens to be mine—I am James Southam."

Bending down he glared at me with eyes which seemed to glow like burning coal.

"What do you mean?"

"I mean precisely what I say. If you choose to examine the contents of my pockets—they are at your mercy—you will find ample proof of the truth of what I say. Besides, I take it that you have had truth of this proof from the contents of the papers."

"The contents of the papers—what papers?"

I looked at him to see if his seeming ignorance of what I meant was real. It appeared to be.

"You and I, Mr. Southam, or Mr. Barnes, or whatever your name is, have been, and it would seem still are, at cross purposes. I take no more interest in your affairs than you take in mine—perhaps not so much. The mention of my name seems to have awoke uncomfortable echoes in your breast, which fact is of the nature of an odd coincidence."

"You are not a policeman, or a detective, or a private inquiry agent, or anything of that kind—you swear it?"

"Very willingly. I am simply a poor devil of a clerk out of a situation. Why you should object to me, or, still more, why you should fear me, I have not the faintest notion."

He hesitated before he spoke again—then his tone was sullen.

"I don't know if you are lying: I expect you are: but anyhow, I'll chance it. I fancy that I'm about your match, if it's tricks you're after. If I let you get up, can I trust you?"

"You can: again I give you my word for it."

He let me rise. When I had done so, and was brushing the dust off my clothes, I took his measure. Even by the imperfect light I could see how shabby he was, and how hollow his cheeks were. He seemed to have shrunk to half his size since that first short interview I had had with him.

"You will excuse my saying you don't look as if you have been living in clover."

"I haven't. I am nearly starving. It is that which has brought me back."

"Why did you ever go? Mrs. Barnes tells me that you are her husband. I should imagine that you had a pretty comfortable birth of it."

He glowered at me with renewed suspicion. "Oh, she has told you so much, has she? What has she told you more?"

"Very little. She has been half beside herself trying to think what has become of you, especially since this affair of Duncan Rothwell."

We had crossed the road and were on the Embankment, walking towards the City side by side. Although I had made the allusion of set purpose, I was scarcely prepared for the effect which it had on him. Plainly, he was a person of ungovernable impulses. He stopped, swung, round, again the knife was gleaming in his grasp, and his hand was at my throat. But this time I succeeded in warding him off.

"What is the matter with you, man? Are you stark mad?"

He was breathing in great gasps. "What name—was that—you said?"

"Surely the name must be a familiar one to you by now. It has been to the front enough in all the papers."

"The paper! What papers?"

"The newspapers, man, of course!"

"How do I know what is in the newspapers? I never look at them. There is nothing in them which is of interest to me. What name was that you said? Tell me if you dare!"

He made a threatening gesture with his knife, seeming to be half frenzied with excitement.

"Duncan Rothwell—the man who was murdered at your wife's front door."

"Duncan Rothwell! Murdered—at my wife's—front door!"

The knife fell from his hand. He gave such a backward lurch that I half expected to see him fall down after it. In an instant, stooping, I had the knife in my grasp. I felt strongly that such a weapon was safer in my possession than in his. He did not seem for the moment to be conscious of what it was which he had lost and I had gained. He stood staring in front of him with an air of stupefaction. He repeated his own words over to himself, stammeringly, as if he were unable to catch their meaning: "Murdered—at my wife's—front door!"

"Where have you been living not to have heard of it? It has been the topic of every tongue."

I could see that he was struggling to collect his scattered senses. He spoke at last as if he were waking from a dream.

"I have heard nothing. I do not understand what you are talking about. Tell me everything."

I told him all that there was to tell. Evidently the whole of it was news to him. He listened greedily, gulping down, as it were, every word I uttered, as if

I had been feeding him with physical food as well as mental. As I noted his demeanour, it seemed incredible that he could have been the chief actor in the tragedy to the details of which he listened with such apparently unfeigned amazement. I had been guilty of an unintentional injustice in doubting him. As I told my tale we leaned upon the parapet—he never looking at me once, but straight into the heart of the river.

When I had finished he was silent for some moment. Then he put to me a question:

"Do you mean to say that nothing has been found out to show who did it?"

"Absolutely nothing."

Unless I erred, he smiled. Had I not done him an injustice after all? Could the man be such a consummate actor?

"And yet you almost saw him killed?"

"Had I come into the hall half a moment sooner I might have seen the murderer in the act of perpetrating his crime."

This time he laughed right out—an evil laugh.

"For goodness' sake, man, don't laugh like that—it makes me shiver."

He was still, with a stillness which, somehow, I did not care to break. A far-away look began to come into his face. He seemed to become lost in thought. When, after a long interval, during which I was sufficiently engaged in watching the different expressions which seem to chase each other across his face, he broke the silence, it was as though he muttered to himself, oblivious of his companion and of the place in which he was: "What a woman she is!"

That was what he said. I caught the words as he uttered them beneath his breath—uttered them, as it seemed, half in admiration, half in scorn. And he again was still.

41

CHAPTER VIII

"MURDERER!"

He would not go home. I spent, I daresay, an hour in seeking to persuade him. I pointed out the injury he was doing to himself, the wrong which he was doing his wife. I went further—I more than hinted at the suspicions which might fall upon him in connection with the Rothwell murder; plainly asserting that it would be the part of wisdom, to speak of nothing else, for him to put in an appearance on the scene, look the business squarely in the face, and see it boldly through. But he was not to be induced. The most that I could get from him was a promise that he would come to the front, to use his own words, "when the time was ripe"—what he meant by them was more than I could tell. In return, he extracted a promise from me that I would say nothing of our meeting to his wife until he gave me leave—a promise which was only given on the strength of his solemn asseveration that such silence on my part would be best for his wife's sake, and for mine. He would give me no address. In reply to my fishing inquiries into the mystery of his personal action he maintained an impenetrable reserve—he was not to be drawn. One thing he did condescend to do: he borrowed all the loose cash which I had in my pockets.

Mrs. Barnes had supplied me with a latchkey; I had been accustomed to let myself in with it when I was late. My surprise was therefore considerable when, directly I inserted the key in the lock, the door was opened from within, and there confronting me stood the ubiquitous new waiter, with the inevitable smile upon his face.

"What are you sitting up for at this hour of the night? You know very well that I have a key of my own."

He continued to stand in the stiff, poker-like attitude which always reminded me of a soldier rather than of a waiter. Not a muscle of his countenance moved.

"I have been accustomed to act as a night porter, sir."

"Then you needn't trouble yourself to act as a night porter to me. Let me take this opportunity to speak to you a word of a sort. What is the nature of the interest you take in my proceedings, I do not know. That you do take a peculiar interest is a little too obvious. While I remain in this house I intend to come, and to go, and to do exactly as I please. The next time I have cause to suspect you of spying upon my movements you will be the recipient of the best licking you ever had in all your life. You understand? I shall keep my word, so you had better make a note of it."

The fellow said nothing in return; his lips were closely pursed together. I might have been speaking to a dummy, except that there came a gleam into his eyes which scarcely suggested that his heart was filled with the milk of human kindness.

When I had reached my bedroom, and, having undressed, was opening my night shirt preparatory to putting it on, there fell from one of the folds of the garment a scrap of paper.

"What now?" I asked myself, as I watched it go fluttering to the floor. I picked it up; it only contained four words, and they were in Mrs. Barnes's writing: "You are in danger."

This, veritably, was an hotel of all the mysteries. Whether the husband or the wife was the more curious character, was, certainly, an open question. For days she had avoided me. In spite of my attempts to induce her to enter into conversation I had scarcely been able to get a word out of her edgeways. Why had she chosen this eccentric method of conveying to me such an enigmatic message? I was in danger! Of what? It struck me forcibly, and not for the first time, that if I remained much longer an inmate of Barnes's hotel I should be in distinct danger of one thing—of going mad!

I had still some papers left to copy, out of the last batch which Mrs. Lascelles-Trevor had given me. I had been accustomed to do my work in her private sitting-room, it being my habit, as I understood it, in accordance with her wish, first to have breakfast, and then to go upstairs and ask her if she was prepared for me to commence my duties. The next morning I followed the ordinary course of procedure, and was at her door, if anything, rather before the usual hour. But instead of vouchsafing me a courteous greeting, as it was her wont to do, she commenced to rate me soundly, asking me if I thought that her time was of no account, since I kept her waiting till it suited me to give her my attention.

I made no attempt to excuse myself, imagining that she was suffering from an attack of indigestion, or from some other complaint which female flesh is peculiarly heir to, contenting myself with repeating my inquiry as to whether she was ready to avail herself of my proffered services. The fashion of her rejoinder hardly suggested that the lady who made it was stamped with the stamp which is, poetically, supposed to mark the caste of Vere de Vere.

"Don't ask me such absurd questions! You don't suppose that I'm the servant, and you're the master. Sit down, and begin your work at once, and don't try any of your airs with me!"

I sat down, and began my work at once. It was not for me to argue with a lady. Beggars may not be choosers, and I could only hope that the infirmities of a feminine temper might not be too frequently in evidence as a sort of honorary addition to the charms of my salary.

That the lady meant to be disagreeable I could have no doubt as the minutes went by; and scarcely had I commenced to write than she began at me again. She found fault with my work, with what I had done, with what I had left undone, as it seemed to me, quite causelessly. I bore her reproaches as meekly as the mildest mortal could have done.

My meekness seemed to inflame rather than to appease her. She said things which were altogether uncalled for, and which beyond doubt an office boy would have resented. That I should keep my temper in face of her continued provocation evidently annoyed her. Suddenly springing out of her chair, she bounced from the room.

"I trust," I said, apostrophising her when she had gone, "that when you do return your temperature will be appreciably lower. In any case, I fancy, Mrs. Lascelles-Trevor, that you and I shall not long stand towards each other in the position of employee and employer. Even by a lady one does not care to be called over the coals—and such coals!—for nothing at all. One had almost better starve than be treated, in and out of season, as a whipping boy."

The papers which I was engaged in copying comprised all sorts of odds and ends, more worthy, I should have thought, of the rubbish heap than of transcription. They were about all sorts of things, and were in no sort of order, and why they should be deemed worthy of being enshrined in the beautiful manuscript book with which Mrs. Lascelles-Trevor had supplied me was beyond my comprehension.

I had finished transcribing one paper. Laying it down, I drew towards me another. It was a letter, and was in a hand which I had not previously encountered. The caligraphy, even the paper on which the letter was written, filled me with a strange sense of familiarity. Where had I seen that carefully crabbed, characteristic handwriting before?—every letter as plain as copperplate, yet the whole conveying the impression of coming from an unlettered man. I had had a previous acquaintance with it, and that quite recently.

I had it—it came to me in a flash of memory!

The writing was that which had come to me in the communication which had been signed Duncan Rothwell. This letter and that letter had emanated from the same scribe. I could have sworn to it. Even the paper was the same. I remembered taking particular notice of the large sheet of post, with the unusually coarse grain; here was that sheet's twin brother!

What was a letter from Duncan Rothwell doing among Mrs. Lascelles-Trevor's papers?

It was my duty to copy the thing. It was, therefore, necessary that I should read it. It bore no date and no address. It began:—"My dearest Amelia." Who was my dearest Amelia? A glance sufficed to show me that it was a love-letter, and a love-letter of an uncommon kind. Clearly, there had been some blunder. Such an epistle could not intentionally have been lumped with that olla podrida of scraps and scrawls. It was out of place in such a gallery. What was I to do?

The question was answered for me. While I still hesitated, Mrs. Lascelles-Trevor reappeared. I said nothing, but I daresay that the expression of my features and the gingerly style in which I held the letter out in front of me, conveyed a hint that I had lighted on something out of the way. Probably, too, she recognised the letter directly she caught sight of it, even from the other side of the room. Anyhow, she came striding forward—she was a woman who could stride—and, without any sort of ceremony, leaning across the table, she snatched it from my hand. For an instant I expected she would strike me—she was in such a passion. The veins stood out on her brow like bands; her lips gave convulsive twitches.

Since it seemed that rage had deprived her of the faculty of speech, I endeavoured to explain the situation by feigning ignorance that there was a situation to explain.

"Do you wish me to copy this letter in the same way as the others?"

My voice was suave; hers, when it came, was not.

"You beast!" That was the epithet which she was pleased to hurl at me. "I might have guessed you were a thief!"

"Madam!"

Her language was so atrocious, and her anger, so far as I was concerned, so unjustifiable, that I knew not what to make of her.

"Where did you steal that letter?"

I stood up. "Mrs. Lascelles-Trevor, you go too far. You appear to be under the, I assure you, erroneous impression that, in engaging a man to fill the honourable post of your secretary, you buy him body and soul to do as you will."

"You smooth-tongued hound! Don't think to play the hypocrite with me, or you will find yourself in custody on a charge of theft."

I looked her steadily in the face—fury seemed to have distended her naturally generous proportions.

"I fear, madam, that this morning you are suffering from ill-health. When you are yourself again, I feel sure you will tender your apologies."

I moved towards the door. But she would not let me go. She placed herself in front of me.

"Don't think that you deceive me! Don't think that your attitudinising can impose on me! If you do, you are in error. I have known you from the first— yes, before I saw you in the actual flesh. I knew Jonas Hartopp as well as you, and when he fell I swore that I would gibbet the wretch who slew him. All this time I have been watching you, the avenger of blood; I have been tracking you, step by step, playing the very sleuth-hound: It only needs a very little to enable me to prove your guilt up to the hilt; and you may be very sure of this, James Southam, that though you seek to hide yourself in the nethermost corners of the earth, I will have you brought to hang!"

Her words were so wild, and the charge with which she sought to brand me such a monstrous birth of a diseased imagination, that the most charitable supposition could be that the woman was mentally unhinged. I treated her with the contempt she merited.

"Possibly, madam, when at your leisure you have credited me with all the vices, you will suffer me to leave the room."

"That is the tone you take up; you sneer, and sneer, and sneer! I foresaw it. Do not suppose that this further proof of your deficiency in all sense of shame takes me by surprise. So black-hearted a villain was not likely to have a conscience which could be easily pricked. You may go—still this once! It will not be for long; your wings will soon be clipped. I shall soon have you in a cage. Be sure of this: I will show you as little mercy as you showed your helpless victim when he had walked into the trap which you had set for him. You had best be careful. And never forget that wherever you go my emissaries keep you well in sight; whatever you do is known to me within the hour. I have no intention of letting the cord which holds you run too loose."

When she stopped to take breath, I bowed. "I thank you, madam, for your permission to leave the room, and do protest that I esteem myself highly honoured, in that you should take so acute an interest, as you say you do, in my humble person."

She let me go, though seemingly not a little against her will. Even at the last moment I should not have been surprised if she had assailed me with actual physical violence. But she retained sufficient vestiges of self-control to refrain from doing that. When I opened the door she caught hold of the handle to prevent my shutting it. As I went out she followed me on to the landing. I, supposing she desired to go downstairs, moved aside so as to permit of her passage. She took no notice of my action, so I went downstairs. As I went, she stood at the head of the flight, observing me as I descended, and she said, in a tone of voice which was too audible to be pleasant for me—

"Murderer!"

CHAPTER IX

THROWN IN HER FACE

I must admit that, in spite of my efforts to keep up the outward semblance of indifference, when I reached the hall I was at a loss what next to do. A man scarcely ever has a passage of arms with an angry woman without suffering some loss of dignity, and that no matter how much in the right he is. I had a mine sprung on me from a wholly unexpected quarter; I had been accused of being an assassin by the woman who, for at any rate one sanguine second, I had fondly fancied was about to play the part of my good fairy; and now, as I was endeavouring with the finest air of conscious rectitude which I had at my command, to remove myself from the lash of her vigorous tongue, she had thrown after me in public that hideous epithet. I was aware that the maid, with eyes and ears wide open, was peeping at me from the banisters above, while standing stolidly at the foot of the stairs was that much too attentive waiter. As he moved to let me pass Mrs. Lascelles-Trevor—I was always fond of double-barrelled names, being persuaded that they were invariably marks of birth and breeding—gave me an assurance that I was still in range.

She addressed the waiter with perfect spontaneity.

"You may let him go, my man, for the present. But his course is nearly run, and he will be in the hands of the police sooner than he thinks."

I did not feel myself entitled to knock the man down because the woman insulted me, though my inclination went that way. I was still less disposed to turn and slang her back again, being convinced that in such a contest I should not be her equal. My impulse was to seek out Mrs. Barnes, as the landlady, and therefore responsible for all that took place in her establishment, and submit my grievances to her. But a glimpse that I caught of her, beating a precipitate retreat into her sanctum, directly she saw me glance in her direction, informed me that such a mode of procedure would be worse than vain. I turned into the coffee-room. Then, feeling that I must go somewhere to cool my brain, I quitted it almost immediately, to sally forth into the street.

I had brought my wares to a pretty market! Disaster seemed to be heaped upon disaster's head. Mrs. Lascelles-Trevor might be mad, but there seemed to be method in her madness, and if she really was possessed by the fixed idea that I was an assassin, though I might not stand in actual peril of my life, I could hardly be in a more awkward situation. No wonder I had felt towards her an instinctive antagonism, even when she had appeared to be most friendly. I was not sure that I had done wrong in not seeking to rebut even the wildest of her wild words with a greater show of gravity. The levity with which I had received them might be urged against me if it came to an arrest.

An arrest! At the mere thought of such a climax I involuntarily stood still. Cold sweat was on my brow.

I remembered what Mrs. Lascelles-Trevor had said about her emissaries being always on my track. For some time past I had had an uneasy feeling that my footsteps were being dogged and that I was being watched. I turned to see if any one was shadowing me now: he would have a bad time of it if I found him. I noted no one whose obvious attentions I could resent. But then I was in the Strand; in that busy thoroughfare the merest tyro could ply his trade of spy without fear of premature detection.

I turned towards Waterloo Bridge, a sudden thought striking me as I did so. I would go for advice to Messrs. Cleaver and Caxton: it was through them, in the first place, I had got into this scrape; it ought to be their business to get me out of it. I went, though I might have saved myself the trouble. They expressed their willingness to undertake my defence, if it came to that, and if funds were forthcoming. But so far from giving me the sort of advice I wanted—advice which would enable me to escape the dreadful ordeal of the prisoner's dock—I could see from their manner, if not from their words, that they thought it as likely as not that I was guilty of the crime which, as it seemed, was about to be imputed against me.

I left them, feeling very little reassured, and sick at heart returned to the hotel. On one point I was finally resolved: under that roof I would not sleep another night. After what had happened in the morning, even Mrs. Barnes would not have the hardihood to suggest that I should continue with her any longer—even as a gratuitous guest.

I went straight upstairs to my bedroom meaning to put the few things together which were mine, and then, and only then, I would have an interview and an explanation with Mrs. Barnes. This was my programme, but, like so many other programmes I had arranged, it was not destined to be carried out.

Directly I reached the bedroom door I became conscious that some one was inside. Supposing it was the maid, who was performing her necessary routine duties, I unceremoniously entered. The person within was not, however, the attendant abigail—it was a man. He lay on his stomach on the floor, with half his length beneath the bed. It was the new waiter. There could be no mistake about the nature of his occupation—I had caught him in the act. So engrossed was he with his researches, that, before he had realised my presence, I had my knee on the small of his back and a stick in my hand.

"As you wouldn't take my friendly warning, take that!"

I brought the stick down smartly on the nether portion of his frame. He had woke to the consciousness of what was happening at last. With unlooked-for agility, twisting himself partially free, he scrambled from beneath the bed, I continuing, as he struggled, to get in my blows wherever I could.

"Stop this," he gasped, "or you'll regret it!"

"I fancy," I retorted, "that the regret will be yours."

He showed more fight than I had expected. It occurred to me that perhaps, after all, the whipping might not be confined to one side only. But my blood was up—I was not likely to allow such trifles to affect me. All at once, just as I was in the very act of bringing down on him the best blow of any, he caught my wrist and gave it a sharp wrench which numbed the muscles of my arm as if they had been attacked by temporary paralysis.

"You fool!" he said. "You don't know what it is you are doing. I am an officer of police, and I arrest you on a charge of murder."

He had taken my breath away with a vengeance. I gazed at him askance.

"It is false. You are one of that woman's spies."

"I am nothing or the kind, as a shrewd man like you ought to be aware. I have had this case in hand from the first. I came here to play the part of a waiter with the special intention of keeping an eye on you—and I have kept an eye upon you, I fancy, to some purpose."

"It's all a lie!"

"Don't talk nonsense. The game is up, my lad, and you know it. The question is, are you going to come quietly, or am I to use the bracelets—I can get plenty of assistance, I assure you, if I choose to call."

"If you can prove to me the truth of what you say, and can show me that you really are an officer of police, I can have no objection to your doing what you conceive to be your duty, though, I declare to you, as there is a God above us, that in arresting me you are making a grievous mistake."

The fellow eyed me with what struck me as being a grin of genuine admiration.

"You're a neat hand—I never saw a chap carry a thing off neater, though it's my duty to warn you that anything which you may say will be used against you. But you've made a slight mistake, my lad—perhaps you didn't think I found it."

He picked up something from the coverlet. It was a long, thin blade, of a fashion which I had never seen before. It had a point of exquisite fineness. Here and there the gleaming steel was obscured by what seemed stains of rust.

"Perhaps it is owing to my stupidity that I am unable to grasp your meaning. This is not mine, nor have I seen it before."

"Haven't you? That remains to be seen. Unless I am out of my calculations, I shall not be surprised to learn that that knife killed Jonas Hartopp. Oddly enough, I found it just as you were coming into the room— inside the wainscoting, in a little slit in the wall which was not half badly concealed, and which was hidden by your bed. I rather reckon that that small bit of evidence will just round my case up nicely."

"If it is true that you found it where you say you did, I can only assert that I do not know who put it there. I certainly did not."

"No? That is a point which must be left open for further consideration. Now I am afraid that I shall have to trouble you to walk downstairs. You perfectly understand, Mr. Southam, that you are my prisoner."

The bedroom door, in the hurry of my entrance, had been left wide open. Turning, I perceived that Mrs. Lascelles-Trevor was staring in at us.

"Your prisoner!" She echoed the fellow's words. "Mr. Southam is your prisoner? Who, then, are you?" She put her hand to her breast as if to control her agitation.

"I am a detective."

"And you have arrested Mr. Southam—for what?"

"For the murder of Jonas Hartopp."

She clasped her hands together in a kind of ecstasy. "I am so glad! so glad! I congratulate you, sir, on having brought the crime home to the real criminal at last." She addressed me with an air of triumph which was wholly unconcealed. "Did I not tell you that your course was nearly run? It was nearer its close even than I thought."

"I am obliged to you for your prognostication, madam, but I may assure you that though I am not the first person who has been wrongfully accused of a crime of which he was completely innocent, I do venture to indulge in a hope that this is the first occasion on which a woman has permitted herself to gloat over the misfortunes of a man who, without having wronged a living creature, is himself friendless, helpless, and injured."

So far from my words succeeding in reaching the sympathetic side of her

—if she had one—she glared at me, if it were possible, more malignantly than before.

"You hypocrite!" she hissed.

My captor placed his hand upon my shoulder. "Come," he said, in a tone which was unmistakably official. "It is no use staying here to bandy words. Downstairs, Mr. Southam, if you please, and mind, no tricks upon the way."

I told him that he need not apprehend anything in the nature of what he called tricks from me. We went downstairs, Mrs. Lascelles-Trevor close at our heels.

"Step into the coffee-room, Mr. Southam, if you please. I am going to send for a cab. Mrs. Barnes!" That lady appeared. "I have effected this man's capture, as I told you that I probably should do."

So she had known all along who he was, and in concealing the fact, in a sense, had betrayed me. And this was the meaning of her futile, eleventh-hour attempt at warning of the night before.

"Let me have a cab at once. And allow no one to enter this man's bedroom until I have had an opportunity of examining all that it contains. I shall hold you responsible."

I saw that Mrs. Barnes's head was nodding like a Chinese mandarin's, and that it was set in motion evidently by the agitated condition of her nerves. The detective perceived that it would be as well for him to repeat his instructions if he wished them to be acted on.

"Now then, Mrs. Barnes, pull yourself together! Let me have that cab."

As Mrs. Barnes moved aside, with the possible intention of taking steps to execute the officer's commands, I observed that some one was standing at her back. It was her husband. He stood just inside the hall door as if he had just come in, and was wondering what was taking place. He was as shabbily and as poorly dressed as he very well could have been. But there was something in his face and in his bearing which, for some reason which I will not stay to fathom, brought good hope into my heart.

"It's you? Thank God!" I cried. "They have arrested me for murder! I hope you have come to help me!"

At the sound of my voice they turned to see to whom it was I was speaking. When Mrs. Barnes saw her husband, without any sort of notice she broke into a fit of hysterics, laughing and screaming and kicking all at once so that the maid had to hold her tightly round the waist to prevent her making an untimely descent to the ground.

But there was one person on whom his sudden appearance seemed to have an even greater effect than it had on Mrs. Barnes, and that was Mrs. Lascelles-Trevor. When she realised who it was who had come so unexpectedly on the scene, she began to stare at him as if he exercised over her the fabulous fascination of the snake. She shrank from before his glance, crouching closer and closer to the wall. She seemed to actually diminish in size. "You!—you!" she gasped. "No!—no!—not you!"

She put up her hands as if to ward him off her. As he made a forward movement, one could see that she shivered, as if in mortal terror.

"And you!" he said, with an intensity of meaning in his voice of which I had not thought it capable. "And you!" He turned to me, pointing an accusatory finger at the woman in whose bearing so strange a metamorphosis had taken place. "If you had told me last night that she was here, I would have solved the mystery for you there and then. Her presence here makes the thing as clear as daylight. It was she who killed Duncan Rothwell. Acknowledge it, you woman with the blood-red hand!"

He addressed her with a gesture of terrible denunciation. His stature seemed to have magnified, even as the woman seemed to have decreased. His face and eyes were blazing. I understood then how it came about that he had mesmerised poor, weak-minded, nerveless Mrs. Barnes.

"No!" wailed Mrs. Lascelles-Trevor. "No! I never touched him!"

"You dare to deny it!" In the man's voice there seemed to be a wonderful resonance, in his bearing a singular air of command. He took from his pocket a box, and from wrappings in the box the ghastly relics which still haunted Mrs. Barnes in dreams. "Here are the four fingers and the thumb, and the palm of your right hand, woman, with which would have made an end of me. Clearly, therefore, it was with your left hand that you murdered Duncan Rothwell. Deny it if you dare!"

As he spoke he threw at her the dreadful fragments. They struck her full in the face.

"I did it! I own it! Don't touch me—not that!" she screamed.

She fell to the ground—as with amazement and, so far as I was concerned, with horror, we stared at her—in what proved to be an epileptic fit.

CHAPTER X

THE JEWEL KING

The story of Duncan Rothwell's murder, when it came to be unfolded in a court of law, proved to be not the least strange of the many strange tales which have been unfolded there. Its turnings and twistings and involutions were many, but briefly summed up it came to this:

The man who had married the landlady of that hotel in the turning off the Strand, and who, in marrying her, had brought such havoc on her head, turned out to be a man with many names. What his real name was, if he ever had one, was never clearly shown. But there had been a time during which the name by which he had been best known to a certain section of society had been that of the "Jewel King." He had been the perpetrator of most of the remarkable jewel robberies which have so much disturbed society during recent years—a scamp, in short, on a truly notorious scale. Jonas Hartopp had played receiver to his thief. These two had been really remarkable men—men of parts which, fortunately for the world at large, are not often found joined in two individuals.

For years these two had been close friends—colleagues—with souls but for a single thought, which thing was plunder, until a woman came between. This was the woman who has figured in these pages as Mrs. Lascelles-Trevor, but whose real patronymic was shown to be rather more plebeian—Amelia Martin. The man who, for the sake of convenience, I will continue to call Mr. Barnes, was in his way a genius, and a little mad. He lived for a long time with Amelia Martin as her husband, without ever having married her. It is probable that during the whole of this period the woman was in a state of daily and hourly terror. He had a pleasant habit of playing tricks with women, particularly mesmeric tricks, of a sort which would hardly have endeared any husband to any wife. It was seriously alleged, for instance, that on a Monday he would throw her into a mesmeric sleep, and leave her quite alone in the house, and in a state of trance, until he returned on the Saturday to restore her, at his leisure—very much at his leisure—to a condition of consciousness. Thus she was continually losing large slices out of her life, under circumstances which no one could describe as wholly satisfactory.

By degrees she transferred her affections to Jonas Hartopp, and with them she decided to transfer herself as well. Mr. Barnes had just made a great coup.

The world will remember the disappearance of the Countess of Crawley's wedding presents. Mr. Barnes walked away from Crawley House with those priceless gems packed comfortably away in his pockets. Amelia Martin persuaded Jonas Hartopp to rob his friend, if, in a little transaction of that peculiar kind, one may speak of robbery. She offered Mr. Hartopp the Countess's gems for nothing if he would take her with them. In a weak moment Mr. Hartopp yielded to temptation. Unfortunately Mr. Barnes detected her in the very act of flight. She struck a blow for freedom—with a knife. The injury which she inflicted was, however, a superficial one. Before she could strike again he had her in a mesmeric sleep. While she was in that state he cut off at the wrist her right hand, the one with which she had tried to stab him. Restoring her, he showed her what he had done. In her agony she vowed that she would turn Queen's evidence and betray him to the tender mercies of the police, let the consequences to herself be what they might. In short, she made herself so extremely disagreeable that, all things considered, Mr. Barnes thought it the better part of wisdom to decamp.

It was while he was in full flight that he lighted on that hotel in the street off the Strand, on the landlady of which he so generously and rapidly bestowed the name of Barnes. He perfectly realised that his friend and his mistress were leagued together against him, and he took it that Barnes's hotel would form a convenient resting-place and cover until such time as he saw his way to crying quits with the pair.

It is here that the odd part of the story begins, having its origin in one of those freaks of coincidence which, after all, are not so common in fiction as they are in actual life, and are certainly not stranger. The *soi-disant* Mr. Barnes had, in his palmy days, taken up his residence for business purposes, of all places in the world, at Dulborough. Finding that there had been a James Southam thereabouts, and conceiving that it would be as well, in case of accidents, that the credit of his misdeeds should stand a chance of being fathered on the real James Southam instead of on the false one, he had not only taken to himself my name, but had actually located himself in the house in which I had been bred and born.

Jonas Hartopp regretted his treachery almost as soon as he had played the traitor. Either he did not find the lady such a good bargain as he thought he should, or, at any rate, not a commensurate exchange for the good offices of his ingenious and profitable friend. He decided after a while to extend the olive branch towards his whilom colleague. It was with that idea in view that he had inserted the advertisement addressed to James Southam, of Dulborough, which had caught my eye. Under the circumstances, when the newly-fledged Mr. Barnes, acting his *rôle* of waiter, heard the stranger on whom he was attending pronounce his quondam cognomen, it was not surprising that he jumped to the conclusion that the Philistines had tracked him to his lair, and that, in consequence, he turned tail and ran.

Amelia Martin, having played the part of traitor herself, was quick at suspecting intended treachery in another. She had an inkling of what it was Jonas Hartopp, *alias* Duncan Rothwell, proposed to do. The pair had a violent quarrel the night before he went to town. She followed him without his being conscious of the fact, on that eventful journey, in a dangerous mood; and in what, doubtless, was a moment half of fear and half of frenzy, she struck him dead. The evidence at the inquest, and the discovery that there was a real James Southam in the world, and that "Duncan Rothwell," therefore, had started on a futile quest, gave her the idea of removing suspicion from herself by attributing the crime to me—which ingenious plan she might have carried to a successful issue, and I been hanged for what I never had the faintest thought of doing, if the false James Southam had not come on the scene in the very nick of time. It was she who placed the knife with which she had done the deed behind the wainscot in my bedroom!

The trial of Amelia Martin for the murder of Jonas Hartopp, during which this tale was unfolded, continued for a week. On her behalf medical evidence was brought to show that she suffered from periodical attacks of mania, during which she could not justly be held responsible for her actions—for which condition of affairs Mr. Barnes's mesmeric experiments had probably something to do. She was sentenced to be confined as a criminal lunatic during her Majesty's pleasure.

Mr. Barnes's suicide in his cell, on the night before he was to be brought to trial—for, in spite of the assistance which he rendered in the case of Amelia Martin, the police, apparently, had no intention of letting him go "scot free"— was the sensation of a "special edition."

"Mrs. Barnes" sold the hotel and retired into private life. At present, I believe, she is residing with some relatives in a corner of far-off Canada. As for me, I still seem very far from being on the road which leads to the making of a fortune; but, at any rate, I am not at present out of employment, and I sincerely trust that the time is very far distant when I shall be.

The End.

MR. ELY'S ENGAGEMENT

CHAPTER I

THE FIRST WOOER

Number Two, Draper's Gardens, the office of Mr. John Ash, dealer in stocks and shares. Time, noon. Mr. Ash, with his hat pushed on to the back of his head, seated at a table studying a letter.

"Whatever women find to write about beats me. A man puts a volume inside two lines. A woman puts two lines inside a volume."

Mr. Ash rustled the letter irritably in his hands. It was a voluminous production, written by a feminine pen, crossed and recrossed in a way which, in these days of cheap paper and cheap postage, none but a feminine pen would dream of.

"However a man is supposed to read it is more than I can tell. I can just make out the opening: 'My dearest guardian,'—yes, dear at any price! And the signature—where is it? I know I saw it somewhere. Yes, of course, there it is—straggling across the date and the address: 'Your affectionate ward, Lily Truscott'!"

He laid the letter down, and thrust his hands into his breeches-pockets, leaned back in his chair, and began to whistle softly beneath his breath.

"I wish I could get some one to marry her—a decent sort of man. Though, upon my word, if this sort of thing is to go on"—he glanced at the letter with a look of mild despair—"I sha'n't mind who it is. She knows I hate letters—that's why she keeps on writing them. If two men can't know each other without one of them dying and leaving the other with his daughter on his hands, no wonder a man likes to keep his circle of acquaintance small. And when the girl's got looks and money, God help the man who's got to stay and mind her! Well, here goes. I suppose I'll have to answer it, or she'll be writing again to-morrow to know if I am ill."

Taking up the letter he regarded it with a look of ineffable disgust.

"What she says I don't know. Rather than decipher these hieroglyphics I'd lose a hundred pounds. Anyhow, here goes to make the best of it."

Drawing towards him a sheet of paper and a pen he began to nibble the end of the pen.

"What the dickens shall I say? How can a man answer a letter when he doesn't know what is in it!"

He began to write, indulging in a sort or commentary by the way.

"MY DEAR LILY,—I have read your charming letter with the greatest interest. (I have! I have!) You are indeed a mistress of the epistolary art. (I hope she won't imagine that's writ sarkastick. Now, what shall I say?) The account which you give of the doings of your neighbourhood (I hope that's safe—it ought to be, women always do talk about that kind of thing) is most entertaining. (Most!) It is with the greatest pleasure that I hear of your continuance in good health. (I wonder if she says anything about her being ill?) I am glad to hear, too, that your aunt, Mrs. Clive, is still in the enjoyment of nature's greatest blessing. (I wonder if she mentions the old girl's name!) Pray convey to her my compliments. (Old fool! Now for something to wind up with.) I envy you your peaceful sojourn amidst summer's scenic splendours. (Not so bad! 'summer's scenic splendours.') Tied as I am to the Juggernaut of commerce, I can, however, but look and long. (I wouldn't live in a place like that for thirty thousand a year.)

"Your affectionate guardian,

"JOHN ASH."

"I think that'll do. It will, at any rate, prevent her writing again to-morrow to know if I am ill."

While he was examining, with a certain satisfaction, this example of polite correspondence, a voice was heard inquiring for him in the office without: "Mr. Ash in?"

When Mr. Ash heard the voice, an acidulated expression appeared upon his countenance.

"Ely! What does the fool want here? It's not so very long ago since I very nearly had to hurt his head."

"All right; you needn't trouble him. I'll show myself in."

The owner of the voice did show himself in. He was a dapper little man, with fair hair and a little fair moustache, the ends of which were arranged with the utmost nicety, and a pair of rather washed-out blue eyes, which could, however, look keen enough when they pleased. He was what might be described as a bandbox sort of man. Beautiful grey trousers fitted over exquisite patent shoes. A spotless white waistcoat relieved an irreproachable black coat. His necktie was arranged in an absolutely perfect little bow. His hat gleamed as though it had just that moment left the manufacturer's hands. He carried a metal pencil-case, and one of those long, thin note-books which gentlemen of the Stock Exchange use to enter their bargains in. A diamond ring sparkled on the little finger of his left hand, and in the button-hole of his coat, backed by a sprig of maiden-hair, was a sweet blush-rose.

This beautiful little gentleman seemed to be satisfied with himself and all the world.

"Surprised to see me, I daresay."

His rather metallic voice did not altogether accord with the radiancy of his appearance. One expected flute-like notes to come from him. His actual tones were sharp and shrill.

"I am; considering that last time I had the privilege of your conversation you were good enough to say I was a thief."

The dapper little man stood before the empty stove picking his beautiful white teeth with his metal pencil-case.

"Well, Ash, business is business, and no man likes to be robbed, you know."

"Is that what you have come to tell me? Because, if so, you can impart the information equally well while I am pitching you through the window."

The little man did not seem at all annoyed. He did not even seem amused. He appeared to be quite accustomed to that sort of speech. He seemed to take it for granted, at any rate.

"Well, no—quite the other way. Fact is, I'm looking for a wife."

"A what?"

"A wife."

"The deuce you are! And do you think I've a selection on view here?"

"Not a selection. You've got one."

"What the dickens do you mean?"

"Come, Ash, you know. It's your ward, Miss Truscott."

Mr. Ash gave a loud whistle of surprise. Then he turned in his chair and stared at the dapper little man. The dapper little man went on, in the calmest, matter-of-fact sort of way—

"The fact is, I'm sick of chambers, and I'm sick of dining at the club. I want a house, and I don't care to take a house unless I take a wife. Why shouldn't it be Miss Truscott, Ash?"

He paused as if for a reply. But if he did, none came.

"There's another thing. You know Rosenbaum?"

Mr. Ash signified assent.

"He wants to plant one of his girls on me. All six of them, so far as I can see. He's always shying them at my head. Besides, he's been hammered twice. If he went again, where should I be, I'd like to know. Not to mention that the whole six of them have got carbuncles instead of noses, and moustaches quite as good as mine."

"I did hear that you were engaged to a Miss Rosenbaum."

"Then you heard wrong; I ain't. Why shouldn't it be Miss Truscott, Ash? I've got something and she's got something. I tell you fairly, if she hadn't it wouldn't do. And if we pulled together, you and I, we might put something in each other's way."

He winked at Mr. Ash. Mr. Ash grinned, and turned aside. He regarded the letter on his desk.

"Have you spoken to her yet?"

"Not a word. I wanted first to have things clear with you. I'll run down to-morrow if it's all serene."

Mr. Ash appeared to be turning the matter over in his mind. "There's no man in England that girl need ask to marry her."

"I'm sure I never said there was."

"Ah, I daresay if you were to take nine men out of ten and heap them in a crowd, she might take her pick out of the lot!"

"If it comes to that, I might take my pick out of a few. Frederic Ely's a man who never need go begging."

Mr. Ash smiled. His smile was scarcely flattering to his friend. He continued to turn the matter over in his mind. Suddenly he got up.

"Ely, I like you. We've had our differences, but as you say, that's because we're both men of business, and like to see the entries on the right side of the ledger."

That was not exactly what Mr. Ely had said but no matter.

"Lily Truscott's a girl in a thousand—in million, sir. I know her—I know her well. There's nothing in that girl's heart which is hidden from me, and that girl's heart's all good, and that's something to say of a girl at this time of day. If she were my daughter, and I were her father, there's no man to whom I should be more willing to give her, sir, than you. Take her, sir; take her! and I wish you joy!"

He turned away, but whether it was to hide a tear or even some deeper sign of heartfelt emotion, is a difficult thing to say. Mr. Ely did not appear much touched.

"That's the time of day, old man. You send her along a line to say I'm on the road; prepare her mind, you know."

If Mr. Ash did not know, at least Mr. Ely winked.

"I'll be up in time. If you write to her now, she'll get it the first thing in the morning, and she'll have time to settle herself before I come. Ta, ta! See you in the house!"

Mr. Ely moved towards the door. Mr. Ash spoke to him just as he reached it.

"How about that Erie syndicate?"

Mr. Ely paused. He stared steadily at Mr. Ash's back.

For some reason Mr. Ash continued with his back turned away.

"You help me with this and I'll help you with that. I can't say fairer than that, my boy."

Apparently Mr. Ash did not seem to think he could, for when Mr. Ely was gone, and the door was closed, he indulged in a little quiet laughter. He reseated himself in his chair and began to nurse his knee.

"I think—yes—I think that will do. Ely's a curious combination; in business matters one of the shrewdest men I know, out of them one of the greatest idiots on earth. However, I think that it will do. I'll just add a postscript to that letter of mine."

He drew the letter towards him, and to the end of it tagged the following—

"P.S.—By the way, a friend of yours—Mr. Frederic Ely—will be with you to-morrow morning—perhaps almost as soon as you get this. He is a gentleman for whose character I have the greatest respect. He will ask my dear Lily a question in which both he and I are deeply interested. I earnestly trust that my dear Lily's heart will answer 'Yes.'"

He scanned the P.S. with admiring eyes.

"I call that neat but not gaudy. None of the awful guardian there. And, upon my word, I don't see why she shouldn't have him; one idiot's as good as another, and if he chooses he can be as good as a hundred thousand pounds to me."

Folding the letter, he placed it in an envelope and addressed it: "Miss Truscott, The Cliff, Shanklin, Isle of Wight." While he was still engaged in this proceeding, the clear, ringing tones of a man's voice was heard in the outer office, and for the second time that morning the door of Mr. Ash's sanctum was unceremoniously opened, and, again unannounced, a second visitor came in.

CHAPTER II

THE SECOND WOOER

A very different visitor this to the first. A tall, stalwart fellow, with a guardsman's chest, a long fair beard which hid his neck, and a huge pair of the most ridiculous moustaches. No bandbox fellow he! Dressed in a shooting suit, crowned by a soft, deer-stalker's hat, flourishing what was a bludgeon rather than a stick in his hand, he seemed hardly the type of figure which is generally to be found in the neighbourhood of Capel Court.

"Hallo, Ash, tracked you down, old man."

His voice was like himself: there was plenty of it. It should have been worth a fortune to him on the Stock Exchange.

"Summers! Whatever brings you here?"

"What doesn't often bring a man to the City—love, and my lady's eyes."

"What!"

Mr. Ash fairly sprang out of his chair. He stared at his visitor with bewildered surprise.

"You may well stare, and stare your fill. I'm worth staring at to-day, for I just don't feel as though I know whether I'm standing on my head or heels. The greatest stroke of luck has happened to me that ever happened to a man before—I've sold my picture for a thousand pounds."

"You've done what?"

"Ah, I knew you wouldn't believe it. It does sound incredible, doesn't it? But it is a fact, though, all the same. I've sold my New Gallery picture, 'A Dream of Love: an Idyll, by William Summers,' for a thousand pounds."

"And have you come all the way to Draper's Gardens to tell me so? It's very good of you, I'm sure.

"It would be good of me if that was all, but it's not; there happens to be more. What does that sale mean? It means that I've made a hit—that I've got a commission for another at the same price—that my fortune is made. I'm a man of fortune, sir."

"I assure you I am very glad to hear it; but I hope you will excuse my mentioning that I still have my fortune to make, and that this is the busiest hour of the day."

"All right, wait half a jiffy, man. Keep yourself in hand, for upon my soul I can't. What does my being a man of fortune mean? It means that I have become a marrying man—a man who has a right to marry. So I'm going to marry."

"I congratulate you with all my heart. Do I know the lady?"

"Well, rather, considering that she's your ward."

"What!"

"Miss Truscott's going to be my wife. I thought I would just drop in and let you know."

"Drop in and let me know! If this isn't the coolest proceeding I ever heard of in my life!"

The amazed Mr. Ash stared at his visitor, who seemed, so to speak, to be laughing all over his face. Then he dropped into his chair, and stared at the addressed letter which lay upon his desk. He appeared to be conscious of a certain confusion of mind.

"Good gad!" he told himself; "just now I was wishing that some one would come along and marry her. This is a case of one's wishes being too plentifully granted. It strikes me there's one too many."

Then he addressed himself to his visitor aloud—

"Really, Mr. Summers, I fail to understand you."

"It's plain enough."

"It may be plain enough to you. You must allow me to say that it is anything but plain enough to me. May I ask when you made what I must call this surreptitious request to my ward for her hand?"

"Oh, that's just the point. I haven't spoken to her yet."

"You haven't spoken to her yet! I understood you to say that she was going to marry you?"

"That's right enough—so she is."

"This may be plain enough to you, but it is really getting still less plain to me. You evidently think that her guardian's consent is not required. May I ask if you think that the lady's is unnecessary too?"

"There are more things in heaven and earth than are dreamt of in your

65

philosophy—I see that plainly, Ash! Don't you know that there is a language more eloquent than speech? That it is possible for a man and woman to understand each other perfectly and yet not interchange a word? We understand each other like that, my friend."

"I should be sorry to say anything which might lessen your self-conceit, but I think you are mistaken, Mr. Summers."

"Oh, no, I'm not."

"But I say you are! Hang it, sir, I never saw a more 'Came, saw, and conquered' style about a man before. If I were you, I would wait for victory to forward your despatch. As it is, I happen to know that Miss Truscott is engaged already."

So saying, Mr. Ash slipped his letter into the inner pocket of his coat.

"What!"

"For goodness' sake, Mr. Summers, don't shout the ceiling down! You will have the people coming in from the street, not to speak of the clerks outside."

"If I didn't know that you meant it for a jest, I should say it was a lie."

"You may say exactly what you please, it won't alter the fact."

"The fact! You call that a fact! I'll go down to Shanklin by the next train, and learn the truth from her own lips."

Mr. Summers made for the door, but Mr. Ash interposed; he was conscious that it would be advisable to induce this impetuous suitor to hasten slowly.

"One moment, Mr. Summers. I am sure you would be unwilling to do another an injury, even unconsciously. If you will restrain your impatience I will endeavour to explain to you exactly how the matter lies."

"How the matter lies? That's just what it does do—it lies! Or some one does, at any rate."

"Mr. Summers, you are a man of honour—we are both men of honour, I trust. Would you have me break my plighted word?"

"Break your plighted word? That depends. If you've plighted your word to break my heart, by George! I'd have you break it, then!"

"Let me remove this matter from the realms of romance into the regions of common sense."

"When you City men begin to talk about common sense you mean something very common indeed."

"Mr. Summers, this is a very solemn subject to me."

"Solemn subject to you! I wonder what sort of subject you think it is to me. Is she going to be my wife or yours?"

"Miss Truscott will be the wife of neither."

"Won't she? By George, we'll see!"

Again Mr. Summers made helter-skelter for the door. Again Mr. Ash made haste to interpose.

"If you will permit me to speak half a dozen consecutive words without interruption, I will make it plain to you that what I have at heart is the interest of all concerned."

"Except me! Never mind, I'll listen. Out with your half a dozen words."

Mr. Summers dropped into a chair in a way which must have been a severe test of its solidity, and brought his bludgeon down upon the floor with a bang. Mr. Ash started. He felt that this was a sort of suitor he had not bargained for.

"The case in a nutshell is simply this. Just before you came there was a gentleman here who made exactly the same proposal you have done. He, too, solicited the honour of Miss Truscott's hand."

Mr. Summers was up like a rocket. Again his bludgeon came down with a bang.

"The devil there was! Confound his impudence! What was the scoundrel's name?"

"The scoundrel's name is immaterial. The point is that I agreed that he should go down to Shanklin to-morrow, and, in proper form, make to the lady the offer of his hand."

"To-morrow, did you? Then I am off tonight."

"Still one moment, Mr. Summers, if you please. You appeared to be so certain of the lady's affection that I was scarcely prepared to find you so alarmed at the prospect of a rival in the field."

"Alarmed! Not I! I will back my darling's truth against the world!"

"Then supposing, instead of confining yourself to words, you prove your faith by deeds. Let this man try his luck to-morrow. If he fails, there is the next day left for you.

"Look here, Ash; when he's failed, will you consent to Lily being mine?"

"If he fails and Miss Truscott gives her consent, then I will."

"Then it's agreed! To-morrow, the beggar shall have his chance! The day after, I'll try mine."

Just then the door opened and Mr. Ely appeared. Mr. Summers rushed to him with outstretched hand.

"Hallo, Ely, haven't seen you for an age! You're looking queer! You ought to try a change of air."

"Think so? To-morrow I'm going out of town."

"Are you? That's odd! The day after I'm going too."

These remarks were exchanged while the two gentlemen shook hands.

CHAPTER III

MR. ELY ARRIVES

Miss Truscott was evidently not in the pleasantest frame of mind. It was unfortunate, for she was the kind of maid one feels instinctively ought always to be in a pleasant frame of mind. Tall, slender, with great, big eyes, sunny hair, and the sweetest smile. The latter, however, was conspicuous by its absence, as she sat at the breakfast-table with an open letter in her hand.

She was at breakfast with her aunt. Mrs. Clive was a precise old lady, who always indoors wore lace cuffs and collar, and the neatest of caps. It was a peculiarity of hers that she was never known to be anything but cool and self-possessed. Sometimes her niece was neither. Then it increased the young lady's sense of aggravation to observe how her aunt's demeanour contrasted with her own—as, for instance, it did now.

"You don't seem to be in the least surprised or annoyed or hurt. You quite take it for granted that I should be insulted."

Mrs. Clive considered for a moment before she answered. She sat bolt upright, her hands in her lap, the model of decorum.

"My dear Lily, the younger generation is impetuous."

Miss Truscott sighed. To be called impetuous under the circumstances of the case seemed almost more than she could bear.

"I write to my guardian on the whole four sides of a sheet of paper to tell him that I must get away from this dreadful place or I shall die, and this is the answer he sends."

She spread the letter out before her on the table and read it aloud, with comments by the way.

"'My dear Lily' (yes, dear at any price, I know), 'I have read your charming letter with the greatest interest.' (Did anybody ever hear the like of that? He read my charming letter with the greatest interest, when I wrote to tell him that I quite believed that I should die!) 'You are indeed a mistress of the epistolary art.' (That is a pretty compliment to pay when you write and tell a person that life is not worth living!) 'The account which you give of the doings of your neighbours is most entertaining.' (Now I never mentioned a single word about anything but the state of my mind!) 'It is with the greatest pleasure that I hear of your continuance in good health.' (When the whole letter was written to tell him that I was nearly dead!) 'I am glad to hear, too, that your aunt, Mrs. Clive, is still in the enjoyment of nature's greatest blessing.' (What nature's greatest blessing is I don't know, but I am sure I never even breathed your name.) 'Pray convey to her my compliments.' (With pleasure, aunt!) 'I envy you your sojourn amidst summer's scenic splendours.' (That is what he says, and I actually told him that I was convinced that if I stayed any longer amidst what he calls 'summer's scenic splendours' I should just go raving mad!) 'Tied as I am to the Juggernaut of commerce, I can, however, but look and long.' Now did you—did you ever hear anything like that? And yet you say the younger generation is impetuous! I should just like to have my affectionate guardian here; I'd let him know what the Juggernaut really was!"

The young lady seemed a little excited, but the elder one was still quite calm.

"You have forgotten the postscript, my dear."

"Forgotten the postscript! Oh, aunty, don't I wish I could!' By the way, a friend of yours, Mr. Frederic Ely, will be with you to-morrow morning, perhaps almost as soon as you get this.' Perhaps the wretch is actually on the doorstep now!"

"Lily, Lily! How can you talk like that!"

"So he is a wretch! But never mind, it's all the same to me. 'He is a gentleman for whose character I have the greatest respect. He will ask my dear Lily a question in which both he and I are deeply interested. I earnestly trust that my dear Lily's heart will answer Yes.' Talk about a woman's postscript! Mr. Ash puts nothing in his letter, and the whole library of the British Museum in his P.S.! Well, aunty, what do you think of that?"

"I congratulate you, my dear, on the near approach of your settlement in life."

Miss Truscott gave a little shriek, and then was dumb. She glared at her aunt as though she could believe neither her eyes or ears. Mrs. Clive went placidly on.

"It is indeed gratifying to learn that Mr. Ash has made his choice."

"Who has made his choice?" asked Miss Truscott between her little teeth.

"One for whose character he has the greatest respect. Such words coming from Mr. Ash are satisfactory in the extreme. You are indeed fortunate in possessing a guardian who has your interests so entirely at heart."

"What are you talking about?" asked Miss Truscott. "Do you think I shall marry this man?"

"Lily!" exclaimed Mrs. Give. "You have such a singular way of expressing yourself. But perhaps"—the old lady smoothed her gown—"perhaps you are a little surprised."

Miss Truscott gave a sort of gasp.

"I am," she said. "I am a little surprised!"

"I suppose we are all when our turns come. I remember in my young days when my dear mother told me that I was to marry Mr. Clive."

"Told you you were to marry Mr. Clive?"

"Yes, my dear. And I remember quite well how bewildered I was at first."

"Didn't you love him, then?"

"My dear, how can you ask me such a question! We were comparative strangers. I had only been acquainted with him about three months."

"Three months! Good gracious! Why, I thought three minutes was long enough to fall in love!"

"Lily, I am amazed to hear you talk so flippantly! It is plain that it is quite time that you had more settled views of life. Among the new responsibilities on which you are now about to enter I trust that you will learn the solemnity of woman's position in the world, and the deference which she owes to the married state."

Miss Truscott laughed. Her laughter was of rather an hysterical kind, as though it were near akin to tears. But Mrs. Clive was shocked. She regarded Miss Truscott with what she intended to be considered as severe disapprobation. Then, with her most stately air, she rose and left the room. Pausing at the door, however, she delivered herself of a final expression of her opinion.

"Lily, I am disappointed in you. I can only hope that Mr. Ely will not have cause to be disappointed too."

When Miss Truscott was left alone she sat quite still, looking into vacancy. The smile about the corners of her mouth was hardly up to its usual character for sweetness. There was a glitter in her eyes which gave them quite a new expression. Suddenly she leaned her face upon her hands and shivered. It could hardly have been with cold, for the sun was shining and the day was warm. Then she got up, and began pacing restlessly about the room.

"Is it a dream? Is it a dream?" Her hands were clasped with a sort of hysteric energy.

"What does it matter! He has forgotten me! What fools we women are!" She took out a locket which was hidden in the bosom of her dress, and gazed upon the face which it contained.

"Willy!"—how softly she breathed the name—"twelve months since you told me that story with your eyes—twelve months ago! Where have you been this weary time! I suppose it was an incident with you. I have heard those sort of things are incidents with men. What a fool I was to take it seriously! What fools we women are! I ought to have known that it was the fashion with Mr. Summers to love and ride away."

She stood gazing at the portrait. All at once something angered her—some recollection, perhaps, of long ago. She snapped the slender chain to which it was attached, and flung the locket on the floor. As if not content with this degradation of her treasure, she placed her little foot upon it and crushed it beneath her heel.

"What fools we women are!"

For a moment she looked upon the ruins she had wrought. The pretty little locket was crushed all out of shape. Then came penitence, and stooping down with streaming eyes she picked the broken locket up and pressed it to her lips; and, still upon her knees, flinging herself face downwards on to the seat of a great arm-chair, she cried as though her heart would break.

"I didn't mean to do it, Willy, I didn't mean to do it; but it's all the same, it doesn't matter whom I marry now!"

She was only a girl: and it is a charming characteristic of the better sort of girls that they will do foolish things at times.

But there was very little of the girl about her when Mr. Ely came; she was the stateliest of young ladies then. The air of having just come out of a bandbox was more apparent about Mr. Ely in the country even than in town. He was one of those very few men who are never seen out of a frock-coat. Throgmorton Street or a Devonshire lane it was the same to him. Wherever he was his attire remained unaltered. But it must be allowed that he was conscious that things were not compatible—patent shoes, top-hat, frock-coat, and a Devonshire lane. So from the Devonshire lane he religiously stayed away. He did his ruralising in centres of fashion where his frock-coat was in place, and not in the equivalents of the Devonshire lane. He was not affected by the modern craze for the country side. He objected to it strongly: a fact which he made plain as soon as he appeared on the scene.

Mrs. Clive received him. She began the conversation on what she fondly conceived were the usual lines.

"How glad you must be to get into the country. It must be such a change from town."

"Change! I should think it is a change! Beastly change, by George!"

Mrs. Clive was a little shocked. The adverb did not fall sweetly on her ear. But Mr. Ely went glibly on. He had a grievance which he wished to air.

"Why they don't have decent cabs at the station I don't know. If there was a live man in the place he'd put some hansoms on the road. Fly, they called the thing I came up in! Fly! I should like to know what's the aboriginal definition of 'to crawl'! And dusty! I left my mark upon that seat, and that seat left its mark on me. I feel like a regular dustman—upon my word I do."

Miss Truscott made her first appearance at the luncheon-table. The meal was not an entire success. This was partly owing to the fact that Miss Trustcott seemed to have gone back into the glacial or prehistoric period, and partly because Mr. Ely still had his grievance on his mind. Mrs. Clive did her best to entertain the company, but in spite of her meritorious efforts the conversation languished.

"And how are things in the City?" She felt that this was the sort of question she ought to ask.

"All over the shop!"

Mrs. Clive started. She felt that the answer was not so explanatory as it might have been. Still she bravely persevered.

"Dear me! I suppose that commercial matters are affected by the seasons." She thought that this sort of remark would go home to the commercial mind.

"Eh? Oh, yes; rather! I should think they were! In fine weather traffics go up all round. Noras have gone up one, Doras one seven-eighths, Trunks are flat: there's a rig-out there and rates are pooled, but this side bulls are in the right hole pretty near all along the line. Bertha's about the only one got stuck."

Mrs. Clive was speechless. She looked at Miss Truscott with imploring eyes. But that young lady was tranquilly engaged with the contents of her plate.

"Poor girl!"

It was a study to see Mr. Ely's face when the old lady made this innocent remark.

"I beg your pardon! What did you say?"

"I said, poor girl! I hope she has done nothing wrong."

"Who's done nothing wrong?"

"The young lady you mentioned. Miss Bertha, I think you said. I am not acquainted with her surname."

Mr. Ely was silent. He was not a man gifted with a keen sense of humour, and was not at all clear in his own mind that the old lady was not amusing herself at his expense. Mrs. Clive, conscious that something was wrong, went painfully plodding on.

"I trust, Mr. Ely, that I have not, unintentionally, said something to hurt your feelings. Is the young lady a friend of yours?"

"What young lady?"

Mr. Ely placed his knife and fork together, with a little clatter, on his plate. Was she at it again? This was more than a man could stand.

"Miss Bertha—the young lady you mentioned."

"Bertha's not a lady."

"Not a lady! Dear me! One of the lower classes! I perceive! Now I understand. Ah, I'm afraid that from them anything may be expected nowadays."

Mr. Ely turned pink, not with suppressed mirth, but with what was very much like rage. For some moments an unprejudiced spectator might have debated in his own mind as to whether he was not about to be profane. But if it were so, he conquered his impious tendency, and adopted another line of conduct instead. He rose from his seat. "If you will allow me, I'll go outside for a change of air"; and without waiting for the required permission he marched through the French window out on to the lawn. The old lady turned to her niece—

"My dear Lily, what have I said or done?"

"My dear aunt, I believe that Bertha, in the slang of the Stock Exchange, signifies the London, Brighton, and South Coast Railway. I suspect that Mr. Ely imagines that you have been amusing yourself at his expense."

Mrs. Clive was aghast.

"Go to him, Lily. Don't leave him alone in his present state of mind. He might return at once to town!"

Miss Truscott rose with her most tranquil air.

"We might survive his departure if he did."

74

But her aunt was shocked.

"Lily, it pains me to hear such language from your lips. You are now approaching one of the most solemn moments of your life. Rise to the occasion, child, and show that, although still a child in years, you have within you the wherewithal with which to make a woman in good time."

Miss Truscott looked as if she could have said something if she would, but she refrained. She left the room without a word.

CHAPTER IV

MR. ELY WOOES

The interview between Mr. Ely and the object of his heart's devotion was not so solemn as it might have been. Possibly that was in a measure owing to what had gone before. But it must be owned that Miss Truscott's mood was hardly attuned to the occasion. We must also, at the same time, allow that Mr. Ely's demeanour was hardly that of the ideal wooer.

"Your aunt seems to have a nice idea of business! I've heard a few things, but she beats all! I thought she was getting at me, upon my word I did!"

This was scarcely the remark with which to open a tender interview. Miss Truscott said nothing. She was seated in a low garden-chair, hatless, her little feet peeping from under the hem of her summer gown. She seemed sufficiently cool just then, but her silence did not appear to be altogether to Mr. Ely's liking. He himself did not seem to be as cool as he might have been.

"I believe, Miss Truscott, that Mr. Ash has told you what's brought me here."

Mr. Ely's tone seemed even waspish—not loverlike at all.

"Indeed!" Miss Truscott just parted her lips and let the word drop out, that was all.

"May I ask what I am to understand by that?"

Just then a fat white dog, of the doormat species, appeared on the top of the steps. Miss Truscott addressed this animal—

"Pompey! Pompey! Good dog! Come here!"

The "good dog" referred to slowly waddled across the grass, and on reaching Miss Truscott's chair was raised to the seat of honour upon that lady's knee.

"Are you interested in dogs, Mr. Ely? If so, I am sure you must like Pompey. He generally bites strangers at first, but perhaps after a time he won't bite you!"

"I'll take care he doesn't get a chance—either first or last."

"Why not? He bit a piece of cloth out of the Curate's trousers the other day, but Mr. Staines says that he doesn't think his teeth quite met in the calf of his leg."

Mr. Ely gasped. His temperature seemed rapidly to increase.

"I did not come here to talk about dogs: and you'll excuse my mentioning that you have not yet informed me as to whether Mr. Ash has told you what I did come for."

"Let me see!" Miss Truscott took out her guardian's letter and referred to it before Mr. Ely's distended eyes. "Hum—hum—Pompey, lie down! There, now Pompey has torn it all to bits!" As indeed the animal had, and was now chewing some of the fragments as though they were a sort of supplementary meal. "What shall I do? Pompey has the most extraordinary taste. It runs in the family, I think. Do you know that his mother once ate nearly the whole of a pair of my old shoes?"

Mr. Ely wiped his brow. He was becoming very warm indeed. He seated himself in another garden chair. For a moment he contemplated drawing it closer to Miss Truscott's side, but the thought of Pompey and his extraordinary taste—which ran in his family—induced him to refrain.

"Miss Truscott, I'm a business man, and I like to do things in a business kind of way."

Mr. Ely paused. He felt that he was feeling his way. But the young lady disarranged his plans.

"By the way, Mr. Ely, have you been up Regent Street just lately?"

"Been up Regent Street?"

"Can you tell me if there are any nice things in the shop-windows?"

Mr. Ely did not exactly gasp this time. He choked down something in his throat. What it was we cannot say.

"Miss Truscott, I'm a business man—"

"You said that before." The words were murmured as Miss Truscott stroked Pompey's woolly head.

"Said it before! I say it again! I wish you'd allow me to get right through."

"Right through what?"

"Right through what! Right through what I have to say!"

"Oh, go on, pray. I hope I haven't interrupted you?"

"Interrupted me!" Mr. Ely snorted; no other word will describe the sound he made. "I say, I'm a business man—"

"Third time of asking!"

Mr. Ely got up. He looked very cross indeed. Pompey snarled. That faithful animal seemed to scent battle in the air.

"Well, I'm—hanged!"

We fear that Mr. Ely would have preferred another termination, but he contented himself with "hanged." Miss Truscott looked up. She allowed her long, sweeping eyelashes gradually to unveil her eyes. She regarded Mr. Ely with a look of the sweetest, most innocent surprise.

"Mr. Ely! Whatever is there wrong?"

Mr. Ely was obliged to take a step or two before he could trust himself to speak. As he was sufficiently warm already the exercise did not tend to make him cool. Under the circumstances, he showed a considerable amount of courage in coming to the point with a rush.

"Miss Truscott, I want a wife!"

"You want a what?"

"A wife! Don't I say it plain enough? I want a wife!"

"I see. You want a wife." With her calmest, coolest air Miss Truscott continued stroking Pompey's head. "Did you notice how they are wearing the hats in town?"

Mr. Ely sprang—literally sprang!—about an inch and a half from the ground. "What the dickens do I know about the hats in town?"

"Mr. Ely! How excited you do get! I thought everybody knew about the hats in town—I mean, whether they wear them on the right side or the left."

Mr. Ely was not an excitable man as a rule, but he certainly did seem excited now. His handkerchief, which he had kept in his hand since the commencement of the interview, he had kneaded into a little ball which was hard as stone.

"Miss Truscott, I'll—I'll give a sovereign to any charity you like to name if you'll stick to the point for just two minutes."

"Hand over the sovereign!"

Mr. Ely was taken aback. Miss Truscott held out her small, white hand with a promptitude which surprised him.

"I—I said that I would give a sovereign to any charity you like to name if you'll stick to the point for just two minutes."

"Cash in advance, and I'll keep to any point you like to name for ten."

Mr. Ely was doubtful. Miss Truscott looked at him with eyes which were wide enough open now. Her hand was unflinchingly held out. Mr. Ely felt in the recesses of his waistcoat pocket. He produced a sovereign purse, and from this sovereign purse he produced a coin.

"It's the first time I ever heard of a man having to pay a sovereign to ask a woman to be his wife!"

"Hand over the sovereign!" She became possessed of the golden coin. "This sovereign will be applied to the charitable purpose of erecting a monument over Pompey's mother's grave. Now, Mr. Ely, I'm your man."

Mr. Ely seemed a little subdued. The business-like way in which he had been taken at his word perhaps caused him to feel a certain respect for the lady's character. He reseated himself in the garden-chair.

"I've already said that I want a wife."

"Do you wish me to find you one? I can introduce you to several of my friends. I know a young lady in the village, aged about thirty-eight, who has an impediment in her speech, who would make an excellent companion for your more silent hours."

"The wife I want is you."

"That is very good of you, I'm sure."

There was a pause. The lady, with a little smile, tranquilly tickled Pompey with the sovereign she had earned. The gentleman fidgeted with his handkerchief.

"Well, Miss Truscott, am I to be gratified?"

"Why do you want me? Won't some one else do as well?"

Immediately the gentleman became a little rose.

"May I ask you for an answer to my question?"

"You haven't asked me a question yet."

"Will you be my wife?"

The question was put in a rather louder key than, in such cases, is understood to be the rule. Miss Truscott raised her head, and for some moments kept her glance fixed upon the gentleman, as though she were trying to read something in his face. Then she lowered her glance and made answer thus—

"Frankly—you say you are a business man—let us, as you suggest, understand each other in a business kind of way. In asking me to be your wife, you are not asking for—love?"

As she spoke of love her lips gave just the tiniest twitch.

"I believe that a wife is supposed to love her husband—as a rule."

"In your creed love comes after marriage?"

"At this present moment I'm asking you to be my wife."

"That's exactly what I understand. You're not even making a pretence of loving me?"

"Miss Truscott, as you put it, I'm a business man. I have money, you have money—"

"Let's put the lot together and make a pile. Really, that's not a bad idea on the whole." It was the young lady who gave this rather unexpected conclusion to his sentence. Then she looked at him steadily with those great eyes of hers, whose meaning for the life of him he could not understand. "I suppose that all you want from me is 'Yes'; and that in complete indifference as to whether I like you or do not?"

"If you didn't like me you wouldn't be sitting here."

"Really, that's not a bad idea again. You arrive at rapid conclusions in your own peculiar way. I suppose if I told you that I could like a man—love him better than my life—you would not understand."

"That sort of thing is not my line. I'm not a sentimental kind of man. I say a thing and mean a thing and when I say I'll do a thing it's just as good as done."

"Then all you want me to be is—Mrs. Ely?"

"What else do you suppose I want you to be? It's amazing how even the most sensible women like to beat about the bush. Here have I asked you a good five minutes to be my wife, and you're just coming to the point. Why can't you say right out—Yes or No."

Miss Truscott shrugged her shoulders.

"I suppose it doesn't matter?"

"What doesn't matter?"

"What I say."

"By George, though, but it does!"

Miss Truscott leaned her head back in her chair. She put her hand before her mouth as if to hide a yawn. She closed her eyes. She looked more than half asleep.

"Then I will."

"Will what?"

"Say 'Yes.'"

"You mean that you will be my wife? It's a bargain, mind!"

"It is a bargain. That's just the proper word to use."

"That's all right. Then I'll send a wire to Ash to let him know it's done."

"Yes, send a wire up to town to let him know it's done."

Mr. Ely moved towards the house. From her voice and manner Miss Truscott still seemed more than half asleep; but hers was a curious kind of sleepiness, for in the corner of each of her closed eyelids there gleamed something that looked very like a drop of diamond dew. Prosaic people might have said it was a tear.

CHAPTER V

MR. ELY DEPARTS

Mr. Ely returned to town on the following morning, and Miss Truscott was an engaged young woman. The interval between the moment of her becoming engaged and the departure of the gentleman was not—we are rather at a loss for the proper word to use—let us put it, was not exactly so pleasant as it might have been.

Although the man and the maid had plighted troth they certainly did not seem like lovers; they scarcely even seemed to be friends. The position seemed to be a little strained. Mr. Ely noticed this as the day wore on. He resented it.

In the garden after dinner he relieved his mind. The lady was seated, the admirable Pompey on her knee, so engaged in reading as to appear wholly oblivious that the gentleman was in her neighbourhood. For some time Mr. Ely fidgeted about in silence. The lady did not appear even to notice that. At last he could keep still no longer.

"You seem very fond of reading?"

"I am." The lady did not even take her eyes off her book to answer him, but read tranquilly on.

"I hope I'm not in your way."

"Not at all"; which was true enough. He might have been miles away for all the notice the lady appeared to take of him.

"One has to come into the country to learn manners."

"One has to come into the country to do what?"

As if conscious that he was skating on thin ice, Mr. Ely endeavoured to retrace his steps.

"Considering that only this morning you promised to be my wife, I think that you might have something to say."

Partially closing the book, but keeping one slender finger within it to mark the place, the lady condescended to look up.

"Why should you think that?"

"I believe it is usual for persons in our situation to have something to say to each other, but I don't know, I'm sure."

The lady entirely closed her book and placed it on a little table at her side. "What shall we talk about?"

The gentleman was still. Under such circumstances the most gifted persons might have found it difficult to commence a conversation.

"Are you interested in questions of millinery?"

"In questions of millinery!"

"Or do you take a wider range, and take a living interest in the burning questions of the progress of revolution and the advance of man?"

Mr. Ely felt clear in his own mind that the lady was chaffing him, but he did not quite see his way to tell her so.

"I'm fond of common sense."

"Ah, but common sense is a term which conveys such different meanings. I suppose, that, in its strictest definition, common sense is the highest, rarest sense of all. I suppose that you use the term in a different way."

This was exasperating. Mr. Ely felt it was.

"I suppose you mean that I'm a fool."

"There again—who shall define folly? The noblest spirits of them all have been by the world called fools."

Miss Truscott gazed before her with a rapt intensity of vision, as though she saw the noble spirits referred to standing in the glow of the western sky.

"I must say you have nice ideas of sociability."

"I have had my ideas at times. I have dreamed of a social intercourse which should be perfect sympathy. But they were but dreams."

Mr. Ely held his peace. This sort of thing was not at all his idea of conversation. It is within the range of possibility to suspect that his idea of perfect conversation was perfect shop—an eternal reiteration of the ins-and-outs and ups-and-downs of stocks and shares. However that might be, it came to pass that neither of these two people went in a loverlike frame of mind to bed. But this acted upon each of them in different ways.

For instance, it was hours after Miss Truscott had retired to her chamber before the young lady placed herself between the sheets. For a long time she sat before the open window, looking out upon the star-lit sky. Then she began restlessly pacing to and fro. All her tranquillity seemed gone.

"I have been ill-mannered—and a fool!"

And again there was that hysteric interlacing of her hands which seemed to be a familiar trick of hers when her mind was much disturbed.

"I have made the greatest mistake of all. I have promised myself to a man I —loathe."

She shuddered when she arrived at that emphatic word.

"A man with whom I have not one single thing in common; a man who understands a woman as much as—less than Pompey does. I believe that selfish Pompey cares for me much more. A man whose whole soul is bound up in playing conjuring tricks with stocks and shares. And where are all my dreams of love? Oh! they have flown away!"

Then she threw herself upon the bed and cried.

"Oh, Willy! Willy! why have you been false? If you had been only true! I believe that I am so weak a thing that if you should call to me to-morrow, I would come."

After she had had enough of crying—which was only after a very considerable period had elapsed—she got up and dried her eyes—those big eyes of hers, whose meaning for the life of him Mr. Ely could not understand!

"What does it matter? I suppose that existence is a dead level of monotony. If even for a moment you gain the heights, you are sure to fall, and your state is all the worse because you have seen that there are better things above."

This was the lady's point of view. The gentleman's was of quite another kind. As he had said, sentiment was not at all his line. When he reached his room, he wasted no time getting into bed. While he performed his rapid toilet he considered the situation in his own peculiar way.

"That's the most impudent girl I ever met."

This he told himself as he took off his coat.

"I like her all the better for it, too."

Here he removed his vest.

"She doesn't care for me a snap—not one single rap. I hate your spoony kind of girl, the sort that goes pawing a man about. If she begins by pawing you she'll be pawing another fellow soon. Oh! I've seen a bit of it, I have!"

Here he removed his collar and tie.

"What I want's a woman who can cut a dash—not the rag-bag sort, all flounces and fluster—but a high-toned dash, you know. The sort of woman that can make all the other women want to have her life; who can sit with two hundred other women in a room and make 'em all feel that she doesn't know that there's another person there. By Jove! she'd do it, too!"

Mr. Ely laughed. But perhaps—as he was a sort of man who never laughed, in whom the bump of humour was entirely wanting—it would be more correct to describe the sound he made as a clearing of the throat. At this point he was engaged in details of the toilet into which it would be unwise to enter. But we really cannot refrain from mentioning what a very little man he looked in his shirt. Quite different to the Mr. Ely of the white waistcoat and frockcoat.

The next morning he took his departure. He had been under the painful necessity of spending one day away from town; he could not possibly survive through two. In fact he tore himself away by the very earliest train—in his habits he was an early little man—not with reluctance but delight: by so early a train, indeed, that he had left long before his lady-love came down. Mrs. Clive did the honours and sped the parting guest. She, poor lady, was not used to quite such early hours and felt a little out of sorts, but she did her best.

"Shall I give dear Lily a message when you are gone?"

Mr. Ely was swallowing ham and eggs as though he were engaged in a match against time. A healthy appetite for breakfast was one of his strong points.

"Tell her that dog of hers is ever so much too fat."

Pompey, who was at that moment reclining on a cushion on the rug, was perhaps a trifle stout—say about as broad as he was long. Still, Mrs. Clive did not like the observation all the same.

"Pompey is not Lily's dog, but mine."

"Ah! then if I were you, I'd starve the beggar for a week."

Mrs. Clive bridled. If she had a tender point it was her dog.

"I can assure you, Mr. Ely, that the greatest care is taken in the selection of dear Pompey's food."

"That's where it is, you take too much. Shut him in the stable, with a Spratt's biscuit to keep him company."

"A Spratt's biscuit!—Pompey would sooner die!"

"It wouldn't be a bad thing for him if he did. By the look of him he can't find much fun in living—it's all that he can do to breathe. It seems to me every woman must have some beast for a pet. An aunt of mine has got a cat.

Her cat ought to meet your dog. They'd both of them be thinner before they went away."

It is not surprising that Mr. Ely did not leave an altogether pleasant impression when he had gone. That last allusion to his aunt's cat rankled in the old lady's mind.

"A cat! My precious Pompey!" She raised the apoplectic creature in her arms; "when you have such an objection to a cat! It is dreadful to think of such a thing, even when it is spoken only in jest."

But Mr. Ely had not spoken in jest. He was not a jesting kind of man.

When Miss Truscott made her appearance she asked no questions about her lover. If he had sent a message, or if he indeed had gone, she showed no curiosity upon these points at all. She seemed in a dreamy frame of mind, as if her thoughts were not of things of life but of things of air. She dawdled over the breakfast-table, eating nothing all the while. And when she had dismissed the meal she dawdled in an easy chair. Such behaviour was unusual for her, for she was not a dawdling kind of girl.

CHAPTER VI

THE WOOING IN THE WOOD

In the afternoon she took a book and went for a ramble out of doors. It was a novel of the ultra-sentimental school, and only the other day the first portion of the story had impressed her with the belief that it was written by a person who had sounded the heights and depths of life. She thought differently now. It was the story of a woman who, for love's sake, had almost—but not quite—thrown her life away This seemed to her absurd, for, in the light of her new philosophy, she thought she knew that the thing called love was non-existent in the world. And for love's sake to throw one's life away!

It was not until she reached a leafy glade which ran down to the edge of the cliff that she opened the book. She seated herself on a little mossy bank with her back against the trunk of a great old tree, and placed the book on her knees. After she had read for a time she began to be annoyed. The heroine, firmly persuaded that life without love was worthless, was calmly arranging to sacrifice as fine prospects as a woman ever had, so as to enable her to sink to the social position of her lover, an artisan. The artisan belonged to the new gospel which teaches that it is only artisans who have a right to live. He was a wood-engraver, she was the daughter of a hundred earls. As a wood-engraver —who declined to take large prices for his work—he considered that she was in an infinitely lower sphere than he: a state of degradation to be sorrowed over at the best. So she was making the most complicated arrangements to free herself from the paternity—and wealth—of the hundred earls.

Miss Truscott became exceedingly annoyed at the picture of devotion presented by these two, and threw the book from her in disgust.

"What nonsense it all is! How people do exaggerate these things. I don't believe that love makes the slightest difference in anybody's life. I do believe that people love a good dinner, or a pretty frock, or ten thousand pounds a year, but anything else—!" She shrugged her shoulders with a significant gesture. "There may be weak-minded people somewhere who believe in love, but even that sort is the love that loves and rides away. As for love in married life! In the present state of society, if it did exist it is quite clear to me that it would be the most uncomfortable thing about the whole affair. Mr. Ely is a sensible man. He wants a wife, not a woman who loves him. That's the royal road to marriage!"

As Miss Truscott arrived at this conclusion, she rose from her mossy seat and shook herself all over, as if she were shaking off the last remnants of her belief in love.

"Miss Truscott!"

She stood amazed, motionless, with a curious, sudden fascination as the sound of a voice fell on her ears. It came again.

"Miss Truscott, won't you turn and look at me?"

She turned and looked, and there was a man. She seemed wonderstruck. A very perceptible change came over her. She became more womanly as she looked: softer, more feminine. The scornful look passed from her eyes and face and bearing. She became almost afraid.

"Mr. Summers! Is it you?"

It was a new voice which spoke, a voice which Mr. Ely would never live to hear. And in it there was a hidden music which was sweeter that the music of the birds.

"Yes, Miss Truscott, it is I."

He held out his hand. She timidly advanced, and he advanced a step, and their two hands met. And their eyes met, too. And both of them were still. Then she gently disengaged her hand, and looked at the bracken at her feet.

"Some spirit of the wild wood must have led me. I have come straight up from the station here. It must have been some curious instinct which told me where you would be found."

"Oh, I am often here—you know that I am often here."

"I know you used to be."

"I think that most of my habits are still unchanged. And where have you been this great, long time? I thought that you would never come again."

"Did you think that? Is that true?"

He leaned forward. He spoke in a low, eager, insistent tone, which, for some cause, made the blood surge about the region of her heart, and made her conscious that new life was in her veins.

"Oh! I did not think of it at all. Out of sight is out of mind, you know!"

"And I have been thinking of you all the time. You have been with me in my dreams both day and night. Your face has stared at me from every canvas which I touched. You were at the end of every brush. Everything I tried to paint turned into you. I thought my heart would burst at the anticipation of meeting you again."

She was silent: for the world she could not have spoken then. This sceptic maiden, who but a moment back was so incredulous of the existence of the thing called love, was stricken dumb, conquered by the magic of the spell woven by this man's tongue and eyes.

"I tried to paint you, and I failed—there are fifty failures in my room! But one night there came to me the glamour of my lady's eyes. At the first dawn of day I stood before my canvas, and all at once, as if it were by witchcraft, I had you there. You shall look at that portrait one fine day, and you shall know that I have you even when you are not near. And so, through all the weary time, you have been there; sleeping and waking I have had you by my side. And you—not once—have thought of me!"

Silence. Then she raised her head and looked at him.

"I have thought of you—at times."

"What times?"

There was a pause before she spoke, as if each was conscious of a fascination in the other's glance; eyes continued looking into eyes.

"All times—I think."

"Lady of my heart's desire!"

He still carried the bludgeon which we have seen he had in Mr. Ash's office. He let it fall upon the ground. He stretched out his two hands, and, as if unconsciously, she yielded hers to his. So they were face to face, hands clasped in hands.

"Love lives no longer now. They tell us that it is only in the fables it is found. Yet I think that they are wrong—nay, it is certain that I know they are —for I love you better than my life!"

Silence. Even the myriad sounds of nature seemed to be suddenly quite still. There was no rustling of leaves, no twittering of birds, there was not even audible the murmuring of the sea. And he went on—

"I pray you tell me—do you love me?"

"Willy!"

That was all she said. Then he stooped and kissed her on the lips. "My dear!" he said.

Then they were still. He did not even draw her to him. He only held her hands and looked upon her face. And she regarded him with shy, proud eyes.

"Why have you been so long?"

"Because I had made myself a promise."

"What promise?"

"That I would earn my prize."

"How could you do that?"

"Ah! how indeed! For, truly, it could not be earned. But when I saw you first I was the laziest of men. Until that hour I had thrown my life away. I told myself that until I had done something to redeem the past, until I had made my mark upon the time, I might not make my petition for the prize."

"Then it is your fault, my friend."

"If there is a fault, it certainly is mine, for I am full of fault. But what especial evil have I done?"

She removed her hands from his, and tapping a pebble with her little foot, she smiled.

"You can never guess."

"Is it so black a crime?"

Suddenly she put her two hands to her face and laughed. But her cheeks were crimson all the same.

"Oh! what have I done? I shall never dare to tell." She peeped at him round the edges of her hands. "Shall you be angry with me, Will?"

"Never, if you call me Will!"

"Do you know— But let me begin at the beginning." She removed her hands, and putting them behind her back, looked at him shyly, and then looked down. "Do you know, I thought that you would never come again." He laughed, and there was something in his laughter made her laugh too. "So I was not happy—for I loved you all the time." He laughed again, and, putting his arm about her waist, drew her closer to his side. "Do you know what happened yesterday?"

"Did the cat drink all the cream?"

"No, worse than that—for we haven't got a cat. Have you forgotten Pompey, sir? Somebody asked me to be his wife!"

"What! Who?"

"Do you know Mr. Frederic Ely?"

"Good heavens! Was he the man?"

"What man? Willy—surely you do not know!"

"So that was what he was coming into the country for! To think of the little beggar's impudence. And I wished him luck, by gad!"

He laughed. But she was still.

"Willy! what do you mean? Do you know all about it, then?"

"Why, it was a bargain, sweet. He was to try his luck, and then I mine. I was so sure of you, you see!"

She released herself from his embrace, and again covering her face with her hands, she shivered.

"What have you done?"

"It was this way; let me unfold the tale. I went to Mr. Ash and told him what you know: how all my life was centred in my love for you. He told me that just before I came another man had brought to him the self-same tale."

"Surely not quite the same? Surely he did not say that all his life was centred in his love for me?"

"No, not exactly that! Yet, sweet, why not? For who shall know you and not love you as his life? But at least another man had come to him who wished to win your hand—that priceless hand! And he had given him his word. So it was agreed that he should try his fortune first, and if he failed—I knew that he would fail!—I should try mine. And if I won—ah, how I longed to win!—Mr. Ash would crown success with his consent."

Silence reigned again. They stood a little way apart, he with his eyes fixed on her face, she with hers upon the ground.

"What have I done?" The words were whispered in an undertone. Then she looked up at him with a sudden fire in her eyes. "Do you know what I have done? I have promised this other man to be his wife."

"What! Good God! Lily! what do you mean?"

"He asked me to be his wife. I said I would. I thought that you were false, you see."

"You thought that I was false! But—it is madness! It is a foolish dream!"

"Do not look so utterly dismayed. You said that you would not be vexed, you know. Besides, now it is another thing."

"Another thing! But—Lily, tell me exactly what it is that you have done."

"I will tell you just exactly what it is that I have done. To begin, then. You see, I have not been happy—ever since you went away."

"You foolish maid! And yet you wisest of them all."

"I waited—oh, Will, I waited such a weary time! I thought that you would write, or—or do something that you never did. And at last I began to think that waiting was in vain. And when I was in the most hopeless of my hopeless moods—it was no further back than yesterday, yet it seemed years ago!"—she put forth her hand and touched his arm, and he laughed beneath his breath —"a letter came from Mr. Ash. He said that Mr. Ely was coming here. I showed the letter to my aunt. She seemed to take it for granted that I would do exactly what my guardian wished me to—as though it were a decree that was written in the skies. So when he came, and asked me to be his wife—just out of spite and wickedness I said I would. He never asked me if I loved him; he never pretended even to love me. It was just a bargain: I was to be his wife."

"My little love! What is it you have done? And now, pray, what is it that you mean to do?"

"I shall write and tell him I have changed my mind."

"Changed your mind! What do you suppose that he will say to that?"

"Why, what can he say? It is like a commercial treaty which is in the air. There are some of the clauses to which I am unable to agree. So I withdraw from the negotiations and refuse to sign."

"One thing is sure: you cannot be his wife."

"Will, I am just like you! I love you better than my life!"

"Sweetheart! Then I have won the prize! I thought that I had won the prize! Will you forgive me my presumption in that I thought that I had won the prize?"

"You should not have kept me so long waiting. It is your fault that I have sinned."

"You shall not have cause again to esteem me false; and observe, fair maid, I had a higher estimate of you."

"Willy! That is unkind!"

Then she turned her face up to his, and when he saw that sweet face upturned and those sweet eyes, what could he do but kiss, not once nor twice, but many times, those sweetest lips? And by this time the two were close together. He had his arm about her waist and pressed her to his breast.

"Do you know that, from my point of view, fair queen, this was worth waiting for?"

"And do you know, sir, that is my point of view as well?"

Then there was silence, and they feasted on the love that was in each other's eyes.

"Lily! Mr. Summers!"

And while they were still engaged in this delectable pursuit, all at once their names were spoken from behind; and turning, they saw that Mrs. Clive was standing in the shadow of the trees.

CHAPTER VII

MRS. CLIVE—AND POMPEY

Mrs. Clive had the faithful Pompey in her arms. That faithful animal was out for exercise, and exercise meant as a rule, to him, being carried all the way. His mistress stared at the lovers, and the lovers, taken aback for a moment, stared at her.

"Can I believe my eyes!"

In her amazement she let the faithful creature fall. Pompey gave a dismal groan. He did not belong to the order of dogs who can fall with comfort to themselves. Where he fell he lay. In the agitation of her feelings Mrs. Clive did not notice the quadruped's distress.

"Lily! Is it possible it is my niece!"

Quite possible, it seemed, and not at all surprising, either.

Recovering from the first momentary shock, Miss Truscott was the most charming niece alive. Removing herself from the gentleman's near neighbourhood, she inclined her body and gave a little graceful curtsey—a prettier curtsey never yet was seen.

"Yes, aunty, it is I." Then she drew herself up straight. "You always said I was your niece." Then she turned to the gentleman. "Willy, don't you know my aunt?"

Mr. Summers laughed. The old lady bridled, but the gentleman, not at all abashed, took off his hat and advanced to her with outstretched hand.

"Mrs. Clive, it is twelve months since I saw you. I am afraid you have forgotten me."

But he was mistaken if he thought that she would take his hand. There never was an old lady with a stiffer mien, and she was at her stiffest now. She had her mittened hands down by her sides, and looked him in the face as though she could not see that he was there.

"I have not the pleasure of your acquaintance, sir."

This was a fib, but there are occasions when fibs must be expected.

"My name is Summers—William Summers. I thought I heard you just now mention me by name. And I, at least, have not forgotten the pleasant hours I spent with you last year."

"Lily, I must trouble you to come with me."

That was the only answer he received to his small compliment. With her most unbending air the old lady turned to go. But the impression she desired to convey was in a measure spoiled. In sweeping round—her action could only be described as sweeping round—she kicked the faithful Pompey; and when the faithful Pompey received that kick he raised a dreadful howl, and that dreadful howl awoke the echoes far and wide. In an instant Mr. Summers had the ill-used creature in his arms.

"Poor Pompey! I am afraid you have hurt him, Mrs. Clive. How well he looks! See, Mrs. Clive, he seems in pain. I'm afraid you must have kicked him in the side, and in his condition that is rather a serious thing. Don't you know me, Pompey?"

It appeared that Pompey did, for, in a feeble kind of way, he put out his tongue and licked his protector's nose. Such a sight could not but touch the lady's heart. Still, of course, it was out of the question that she should unbend.

"I must trouble you, sir, to let me have my dog."

"Permit me to carry him for you towards the house. I'm sure he is in pain —see how still he is."

If stillness were a sign of pain, then the faithful beast must have been pretty constantly in pain, for motion—or emotion—of any sort was not in Pompey's line. Mrs. Clive would have grasped the subterfuge if she had been left alone, but her perfidious niece came to the gentleman's aid. She began to stroke and caress the faithful beast.

"Poor Pompey! Poor 'ickle Pompey, then! I hope he has not broken any bones. Do you think it is his ribs?"

Miss Truscott's back was turned to Mrs. Clive. If the aunt had seen the way in which her niece glanced under her long eyelashes at the gentleman in front of her she would have seized the animal and marched away.

"I scarcely think it is his ribs."

It was not probable, considering how they were swathed in fat.

"Perhaps it is his leg."

"I hope that it is not."

Mr. Summers threw such a tone of doubt into this expression of his hopes that Mrs. Clive's heart gave quite a jump. Her Pompey's leg! Broken! And by her! But she was not by any means going to give in yet. There was the bearded gentleman holding the wheezing quadruped as though it were the most precious thing on earth, and there was her niece very close in front of him. All her sense of moral rectitude was up in arms.

"Lily! I am surprised at you!"

"Surprised at me, aunty! Why? Because you have broken Pompey's leg? I didn't do it, it was you. Supposing he should die? You know what a delicate constitution he always had."

"It is quite possible the injury is less serious than we suppose"; this the gentleman suggested in a consoling kind of way, "though"—here some one gave the dog a pinch, and the dog gave expression to his feelings in a howl —"though decidedly he seems in pain. I think that I had better go on with him straight to the house."

"Lily! I insist upon your coming here."

Miss Truscott did as she was told. With meek face and downcast eyes she fell in decorously by the old lady's side. Mr. Summers, ignored and snubbed, but still triumphant, bore Pompey away in front.

"Lily, what is the meaning of all this?"

"I think you must have let Pompey fall, and then have kicked him when he fell. I cannot see how you can have done it; you are so careful as a rule."

"I am not speaking about the dog; you know that very well. I am speaking of the—the extraordinary scene I interrupted."

"Willy was telling me that he loved me."

"Willy was telling you what! And who is Willy, pray?"

"Willy is Mr. Summers's Christian name."

"Lily, are you stark, raving mad? Have you forgotten what happened yesterday? Are you aware that it is not four-and-twenty hours since you promised Mr. Frederic Ely to be his wife?"

"Yes, auntie; but I have changed my mind."

"You have—what?"

"I have changed my mind."

Mrs. Clive was so overcome that she sank down on a grassy bank which they were passing. It was a thing she had not done for years. She was always under the impression that the grass was damp—even when it burned you as you touched it with the palm of your hand.

"Lily, either you are mad or I must be. Changed your mind! Do you think that in such a matter it is possible for a woman to change her mind?"

"It would seem to be, wouldn't it? Especially when you look at me."

"You treat it as a jest! The most astounding behaviour I ever heard of! I don't wish to forget myself if you have done so; I simply call it the most astounding behaviour I ever heard of! A niece of mine!"

"Perhaps that's it. I—I have such a remarkable aunt."

The temptation was irresistible, but the effect was serious. For some moments Mrs. Clive sat speechless with indignation. Then she rose from the mossy bank and walked away without a word. Left behind, Miss Truscott covered her face with her hands and laughed—a little guiltily, it seemed. Then she went after. So the march to the house resolved itself into a procession of three.

CHAPTER VIII

MR. ROSENBAUM'S SIX DAUGHTERS

In the meantime Mr. Ely was dreaming of his love. It sounds contradictory at first, bearing in mind that he was not a man of sentiment; but the fact was that in his case absence made the heart grow distinctly fonder. By the time he reached Ryde Miss Truscott occupied his thoughts to the exclusion of all else; he never even troubled himself about the purchase of a paper—which was fortunate, for at that hour none had yet arrived from town, and to him the local prints were loathsome. All the way on the boat he dreamed—yes, literally dreamed—of the girl he left behind him. More than once, incredible though it may appear, he sighed.

"She don't care for me a snap, not a single rap, by Jove she don't!"

He sighed when he said this, for, for some occult reason, the idea did not seem to amuse him so much as it had done last night.

"I don't know why she shouldn't, though. Perhaps she thought I didn't want her. More I didn't then, though I don't see why she shouldn't if I did. I know how to make a girl like me as well as any man—look at the Rosenbaums!"

He sighed again. It was "look at the Rosenbaums," indeed! When he thought of those six young women, with their well-developed noses and the fringe of hair upon their upper lips, and of their twice-hammered father, and then of Miss Truscott, that vision of a fair woman, with her noble bearing, her lovely face, and her wondrous eyes, the contrast went deeply home. He felt that he was a lucky—and yet not altogether a lucky—man.

"She's going to be my wife, that's one thing, anyhow."

The Isle of Wight is a great place for honeymoons. It lends itself naturally to couples in a certain phase of their existence. Such a couple were on board the boat with Mr. Ely. Their demeanour was tender towards each other.

"Couple of idiots!" said Mr. Ely to himself as he observed this pair; "it makes a man feel ill to look at them!"

She was a pretty girl, and he was not an ugly man; she hung upon his arm and looked into his eyes. It was plain the honeymoon was not yet done for them. In spite of his disgust, Mr. Ely found himself thinking, almost unconsciously, of another figure and of another pair of eyes—of that other figure hanging upon his arm, and of that other pair of eyes looking into his. He sighed again.

"She doesn't care for me a snap, by Jove!"

Instead of amusing him, it seemed that this reflection began to give him pain. The little man looked quite disconsolate.

"I'll make her, though! I will! If—if it costs me a thousand pounds!"

He had been on the point of stating the cost he was willing to incur at a much higher sum than this. He had been on the very verge of saying that he would make her care for him if it cost him every penny he had. But prudence stepped in, and he limited the amount to be squandered to a thousand pounds, which was not so bad for a man who did not believe in sentiment. But a singular change had come over him between Shanklin and Stokes Bay.

The change was emphasised by a little encounter which he had with a friend in the train. He had taken his seat in the corner of a carriage, when the door was darkened by a big, stout man, who was all hair and whiskers and gorgeous apparel.

"What, Ely! My boy, is it bossible it is you!"

"Rosenbaum! What the devil brings you here?"

"Ah! what the teffel is it brings you?"

Mr. Rosenbaum spoke with a decidedly German accent. He settled himself in the seat in front of Mr. Ely, and beamed at him, all jewellery and smiles. It was as though some one had applied a cold douche to the small of Mr. Ely's back. He was dreaming of the sweetest eyes, and his too-friendly six-daughtered friend—the man who had been hammered twice!—appeared upon the scene. It was a shock. But Mr. Rosenbaum seemed beamingly unconscious of anything of the kind. The train started, and he began a conversation—which rather hung fire, by the way.

"It is some time since we have seen you in Queen's Gate."

Queen's Gate was where Mr. Rosenbaum resided. After each "hammering"—mysterious process!—he had moved into a larger house. It had been first Earl's Court, then Cromwell Road, and now Queen's Gate.

"Been so much engaged."

Mr. Rosenbaum was smoking a huge cigar, and kept puffing out great clouds of smoke. Mr. Ely was engaged on a smaller article, which scarcely produced any smoke at all. They had the compartment to themselves; Mr. Ely would rather have seen it full. He knew his friend.

"Miriam has missed you."

Miriam was the eldest of the six: the one whose nose and moustache were most developed; a sprightly maiden of thirty or thirty-one. "So has Leah."

Leah was a year or so younger than her sister, and quite as keen.

Mr. Ely drew in his lips. He had once played cards with Miss Leah Rosenbaum, and detected her in the act of cheating. He admired the woman of business, but regretted his eighteenpence.

"I've no doubt she has."

"That's a fine girl, Leah! A smart girl, too." Mr. Ely had not the slightest doubt of her "smartness," not the least. "She'll be a fortune to any man. She's very fond of you."

Mr. Ely was certainly not fond of her, but he could scarcely say so to her father's face. So he kept still.

"Rachel, she miss you too."

Silence. Mr. Ely saw plainly that he was going to be missed by all the six. Since he could not escape from the train while it was travelling at the rate of forty miles an hour, the only course open was to sit still and say as little as he could. He knew his friend too well to suppose that anything he could say would induce him to turn the conversation into other channels. The fond father went blandly on.

"She say you gave her a little gift, eh? That so?"

"Never gave her anything in my life."

"No! She says you gave her a lock of your hair; it was little to you, it was much to her. Rachel, she treasures up these little things. She show it me one day; she says she keep it here."

Mr. Rosenbaum patted his waistcoat in the region where his heart might anatomically be supposed to be.

"I tell you what it is, Rosenbaum, your girls are like their father, smart."

"We're not fools," admitted Mr. Rosenbaum.

"One night, when I was asleep on the couch in that back room of yours in Cromwell Road—before you failed last time"—it is within the range of possibility that this allusion was meant to sting, but Mr. Rosenbaum smoked blandly on—"that girl of yours cut off some of my hair, and drew blood in doing it, by George!"

"Ah! she says you give it her—from sympathy, my friend. She admire you very much, that girl."

Mr. Ely kept silence. If there was any one of the six he disliked more than the others it was the young lady whom her father said admired him very much —Miss Rachel Rosenbaum. Some fathers, if they had had the names of three of their daughters received in this rather frigid way, would have changed the subject perhaps. But if Mr. Rosenbaum had not been a persevering man, his address would not have been Queen's Gate. Besides, Mrs. Rosenbaum was dead, and he had to act the parts of mother and father too. And there were six.

"Judith, she miss you too."

This was the fourth; there still were two to follow. Mr. Ely resolved to have a little plunge upon his own account.

"Doing anything in Unified?"

Mr. Rosenbaum looked at him, puffed out a cloud of smoke, and smiled. "I say, Judith, she miss you too."

"And I said, 'Doing anything in Unified?'"

Mr. Rosenbaum leaned forward and laid his great, fat, jewelled hand on Mr. Ely's knee. "Now, my friend, there is a girl for you; plump, tender—what an eye!"

"And what a nose! And a moustache!" was on Mr. Ely's lips, but he refrained.

"That girl just twenty-four, and she weigh a hundred and seventy pound— she do credit to any man. And, my goodness, how she is fond of you, my boy!"

A vision passed before Mr. Ely's mental eye of the girl whom he had left behind. And then he thought of the young lady whose chief qualification was that she weighed a hundred and seventy pounds at twenty-four.

"She not a worrying girl, that Judith; that's the sort of wife for a man to have who wants to live an easy life. She let him do just what he please, and never say a word."

Mr. Ely fidgeted in his seat. "I say, Rosenbaum, I wish you'd try some other theme."

Mr. Rosenbaum held up his fat forefinger, with its half a dozen rings, and wagged it in Mr. Ely's face. "But the great point is Sarah, my good friend; there is something between you and she."

"What the dickens do you mean?"

"Oh! you know what I mean. What passed between you on the river that fine day?"

"What fine day?"

"What fine day! So there has been more than one! That I did not know; the one it was enough for me."

"And upon my word, with all due respect to Miss Sarah Rosenbaum, it was enough for me."

"You did not kiss her, eh? You did not kiss her that fine day?"

"I don't know if I kissed her or she kissed me. I say, Rosenbaum, those girls of yours don't seem to keep many secrets from their father."

"That is as good a girl as ever lived; you will do justice to her, eh?"

"I hope I should do justice to every girl."

"So! That is it! You would marry half a dozen, perhaps!"

"By George, I don't believe you'd offer any objection if I wanted to!"

Mr. Rosenbaum sat back in his seat. Apparently this observation did go home. He appeared to reflect, but he showed that he was by no means beaten by suddenly discovering a fresh attack.

"My good friend, you think you are a clever man. I allow you are no fool, but you have met your match in me."

In his secret heart Mr. Ely was quite willing to allow the fact.

"You have played with my six daughters—very good! You have trifled with their hearts. I say not any word, but there is one of them you must marry, and Ruth is she."

Mr. Ely was silent. He kept his eyes cast down. Mr. Rosenbaum, on the other hand, kept his eyes fixed upon his good friend's face.

"Come, I am her father. When is it to be?"

Then Mr. Ely did look up. The two friends' glances met; Mr. Ely certainly did not flinch.

"It won't do; try some other lay."

"What you mean—try some other lay?"

"Mean what I say."

"You never asked her to marry you?"

"I swear I never did."

"You never gave her to understand that you wished her for your wife, eh?"

"I'm not responsible for her understanding."

"So—that is it!—I see! Griffith of Tokenhouse Yard is your solicitor—not so?"

Mr. Rosenbaum took out a note-book and a pencil-case.

"What's it matter to you?"

"My good friend, it matters this. Before we reach Waterloo you tell me the day on which you marry Ruth, or to-morrow a writ issues for breach of promise."

"Issue fifty writs for all I care."

"You have played hanky-panky with my six daughters, but we have you on the last; at least, we'll see."

"I guess we will. Take my advice, Rosenbaum, and don't you be a fool. I never asked your daughter in my life to marry me."

"We'll talk of that a little later on. There is a letter and some other little things which will make a sensation when they are produced in Court. You understand that it is my duty to see that you do not break my daughter's heart."

"Which of them? All six?"

"At present it is with Ruth we are concerned."

"Oh, Ruth be hanged!"

With that observation the conversation closed. The remainder of the journey passed in silence. But when they reached Waterloo Mr. Rosenbaum remarked—

"Well, my friend, what is it to be? Will you name the day?"

"Name your grandmother!" Mr. Ely courteously rejoined. And with that courteous rejoinder he left the train.

CHAPTER IX

MR. ELY HAS A LETTER

Mr. Ely took a cab into the city. On the road he stopped to buy a ring. He was the kind of man whose determination is intensified by opposition. He had been half in love with Miss Truscott before he met his German friend; now, in his own peculiar way, he was quite. Miss Ruth Rosenbaum was the youngest and most prepossessing of the six, and that there had been certain passages between them he was well aware. But in any case her father's attempt to force his daughter down his throat would have had the effect of making him fly off at a tangent in quite another direction. Now the effect it had upon him was to send him off helter-skelter to purchase Miss Truscott an engagement-ring. But he was the man of business even then. The jeweller found some difficulty in meeting his requirements. What Mr. Ely wanted was an article of the greatest value at the smallest cost. For instance, for a ring priced at a hundred and fifty guineas he offered fifteen pounds—and this with such an air of making a first-rate bid that the tradesman did not know whether to treat it as an insult or a jest. Finally he expended twenty pounds, and had his value for it, rest assured.

Directly he entered the Stock Exchange he encountered Mr. Ash.

"I had your wire," began that gentleman. "I congratulate you, my dear boy."

"Yes." Mr. Ely looked the other straight in the face, which was a trick he had when there was something which he particularly wished to say. Then he slipped his arm through Mr. Ash's, and drew that gentleman aside. "She's a fine girl, Ash—finer than I thought she was. Finest girl in England, in the world, by George she is!"

Mr. Ash was a little surprised at his friend's enthusiasm. But he let no sign of this escape him.

"She's a good girl too, my boy."

"Best girl ever yet I came across."

"And she's true—true as a die."

"Truer—truest girl ever yet I saw."

"And when she says she loves a man—" Mr. Ash paused. He glanced at his friend. Mr. Ely gave no sign. "When she says she loves a man, you may be quite certain that she does."

Mr. Ely looked down at his toes, then up at Mr. Ash.

"I've bought the ring."

"What! The wedding-ring!"

"The wedding-ring! Good gad, no! I never thought of that. It's the engagement ring I've got."

"The other one comes after, eh?"

"I gave twenty sovereigns for it."

"That's a pile." What the smile meant in Mr. Ash's eyes it would be difficult to say.

"He wanted forty-five. I beat him down. Said I'd seen its own brother at Attenborough's for ten." There was a pause. Then Mr. Ely began again. "I say, Ash, when do you think the wedding could come off?"

"In a hurry? Well, what do you say to twelve months, my boy?"

"Twelve months! Twelve months be hanged! A month's enough for me."

"A month! The girl won't have time to turn herself round. And you've a house to take, and all the rest of it."

"You say the word, and I'll have a house by to-morrow night, and get it furnished in a week."

"But, my dear boy, you don't seem to be aware that the lady generally has a voice in that kind of thing."

"You say a month, and I'll make it right with her."

"You may marry her to-morrow for all I care.

"I should like to marry her to-morrow," said Mr. Ely candidly; "but—I suppose it'll have to be a month."

But even a month was not an impassable space of time. Mr. Ely reflected that there were a good many things which must be done—it should be a lunar month, he decided in his own mind—his time would be much occupied, the days would quickly pass, and then—then the maid with the big eyes, the finest girl in the world, the best and the truest, would be his bride.

His happiness was consummated on the following morning. It had never occurred to him to suggest that there should be any correspondence. He was not a man who was fond of writing himself, and a love-letter—the idea of a sane man writing a love-letter!—was an idea which up to the present moment had never entered his mind. And that in spite of a certain unfortunate document which was in the possession of Miss Ruth Rosenbaum. So when he found upon his breakfast table the following morning a large square envelope, addressed to "Frederic Ely, Esq." in an unmistakably feminine hand, the postmark of which was Shanklin, his heart gave quite a jump.

It was from Miss Truscott, as sure as fate: the first letter from his love?

CHAPTER X

THE AMAZING CONTENTS OF
MR. ELY'S LETTER

Mr. Ely played with that letter as a cat plays with a mouse. It was a tender morsel, a *bonne bouche*, which must not be hastily dismissed. He turned it over and over, examining first the superscription, the bold, flourishing hand in which she had penned his name—how well it looked; the first time his name had been inscribed by her! Then he examined the reverse—the monogram. He could make it out quite well—L. T.—Lily Truscott. He blushed as he caught himself in the act of raising the magic letters to his lips. Then he laid it down in a prominent position in front of his plate, and studied the exterior as he began to eat.

"I wonder what she has to say!" Ah, what! "I wonder if—if she's come round to my point of view? Got—got spoony, and—and all that. By George, I hope she has!" What with the food he had in his mouth, and the sigh, he was almost choked. "I think every woman ought to love the man she's going to marry. I love her—I know I do."

He began to know that fact too well. The man who had had nothing to do with sentiment was painfully conscious that he was on the point of becoming the most sentimental of men.

"I mismanaged the affair all through. I ought to have told her that I loved her. How can a man expect a girl to love him if she don't believe that he loves her? Perhaps she has written to say that she can conceal the fact no longer: that she loves me whether I want her to or don't. By George! I hope she has."

He feasted his eyes again upon the envelope, and helped himself to another serving of ham and eggs.

"I thought her behaviour was a trifle cold. It was that beastly dog that did it. How can a man make himself agreeable to a woman when there's a dog ready to bite his nose off sitting on her knee? Still, I thought her behaviour was a trifle cold. She didn't seem to pay much attention to what I had to say; I believe she would have preferred to read; and when she did begin to talk she was taking pot-shots at one all over the place, as it were."

He sighed, and took another egg.

"And when I asked her to marry me I might have been asking her to take a tart; she didn't seem to be interested in the least. She was most uncommon anxious to treat the thing in a business-like kind of way. I oughtn't to have been so particular about saying I was a business man. That was a mistake; I know it was."

He sighed again. He put down his knife and fork.

"By George, if she writes to say she loves me, I—I'd give a hundred pounds!"

He took the letter in his hands.

"I wonder if she does!"

In his anxiety he rose from his seat and began to pace the room, holding the letter tightly in his hand. He paused before the mantelshelf and regarded himself in the glass.

"Well, upon my word, I never thought that I should come to this—I never did. Here's all the papers, and goodness knows what news from Paris, and I haven't looked at one, and don't want to neither, that's the truth. If she's only written to say she loves me, whether I want her to or don't, I—I'd give a thousand pounds. Here goes! I can't stand fooling here all day! Goodness knows what the state of things in the City may be."

He was about to tear the envelope open with his finger. He changed his mind.

"She may have written something on the flap. I'd better use a knife."

He used a knife. To see him use it, opening an envelope might have been the most delicate operation on earth.

"Now for it!" He heaved the greatest sigh of all. "By George, if it's only to confess her love!"

He seated himself at the table with the letter spread out in front of him. It might have been as fragile as it was priceless to observe the ginger way in which he opened it and spread it out. Then he arrayed himself for its perusal with as much precision as though it were some formal and rather complicated revelation just to hand from the gods.

"'Dear Mr. Ely' (I say! She might have said 'Dear Fred,' or even 'Frederic'! 'Dear Mr. Ely'! It's rather a stiffish way of writing to the man you're going to marry, don't you know.) 'Just a line with reference to what passed between us yesterday. I have changed my mind. I thought it better to let you know at the earliest possible moment. It is quite impossible for me to be your wife. The fact is, I am going to marry Mr. Summers instead. Yours truly, Lily Truscott.'"

Mr. Ely read this note through without, in his astonishment, being in the least able to grasp its meaning.

"What—what the blazes is all this!" He ploughed through it again. "'Dear Mr. Ely' (it's evidently meant for me), 'just a line with reference to what passed between us yesterday'! (What passed between us yesterday—what's she mean? She hasn't put a date; I suppose she means my asking her to be my wife. That's a pretty good way of referring to it, anyhow.) 'I have changed my mind!' (Oh, has she? About what? It didn't strike me she had a mind to change.) 'I thought it better to let you know at the earliest possible moment'! (If she had only told me what it was she thought it better to let me know, it would have been perhaps as well. If this is a love-letter, give me the other kind of thing.) 'It is quite impossible for me to be your wife.' (What—what the blazes does she mean?) 'The fact is, I am going to marry Mr. Summers instead'!"

Mr. Ely's jaw dropped, and he stared at the letter as though it were a ghost.

"Well—I'm—hanged!' The fact is, I am going to marry Mr. Summers instead.' That takes the cake!' Yours truly, Lily Truscott.'—If that isn't the sweetest thing in love-letters ever yet I heard of!"

Quite a curious change had come over Mr. Ely. If we may be forgiven a vulgarism which is most expressive—he seemed to have been knocked all of a heap. His head had fallen forward on his chest, one limp hand held Miss Truscott's letter, the other dangled nerveless by his side.

"And I gave twenty pounds for an engagement-ring!"

They were the first words in which he gave expression to the strength of his emotion.

"Good Lord, if I had given him what he asked, and stumped up forty-five!"

The reflection sent a shudder all through his frame. The horror of the picture thus conjured up by his imagination had the effect of a tonic on his nerves, it recalled him to himself.

"I'll have another read at this. There isn't much of it, but what there is requires a good deal of digesting."

He pulled himself together, sat up in his chair, and had another read.

"'Dear Mr. Ely' (yes, by George, dear at any price, I'll swear! Like her impudence to call me 'dear'! I wonder she didn't begin it 'Sir'), 'just a line with reference to what passed between us yesterday.' (That is, I think, about the coolest bit I ever heard of. Quite a casual allusion, don't you know, to a matter of not the slightest importance to any one, especially me. That young woman's graduated in an establishment where they teach 'em how to go.) 'I have changed my mind!' (That's—that's about two stone better than the other. She's changed her mind! Holy Moses! About something, you know, about which we change our minds as easily and as often as we do our boots.) 'I thought it better to let you know at the earliest possible moment.' (She certainly has done that. Unless she had changed her mind before she had made it up, she could scarcely have let me know it sooner. She might have wired, to be sure! But perhaps she never thought of that.) 'It is quite impossible for me to be your wife.' (It is as well that the explanation follows immediately after, or echo would have answered 'Why?') 'The fact is, I am going to marry Mr. Summers instead.' I suppose there never was a larger amount of meaning contained in a smaller number of words. Among the remarkable women the world has seen the record's hers; she is certainly unique."

Rising from his seat, he put the letter back in the envelope, and placed the envelope within his letter-case.

"I'll take that letter up to Ash; I'll have a word to say to him. I wonder if he knows what sort of a ward he's got? That's the best and truest girl alive; a woman whose word is just her bond; who, when she says a thing, sticks to it like glue. And to think that I spent twenty pounds on an engagement-ring!"

He put his hands into his trousers pockets. He balanced himself upon his toes and heels.

"Twenty pounds for an engagement-ring! I wonder how much Mr. Summers intends to pay?"

The reflection angered him.

"By George, I'll let her know if she's going to pitch me overboard quite so easily as that. I'll make her marry me, or I'll know the reason why."

When he left for the City his first business was to pay a visit to Mr. Ash. He dismissed the cab at the corner of Throgmorton Street. He had not taken half a dozen steps along that rather narrow thoroughfare when a hand was laid upon his shoulder; turning, he saw Mr. Rosenbaum.

"My good friend, I have a little paper here for you."

And Mr. Rosenbaum deftly slipped a paper into his good friend's hand.

"Rosenbaum! What's this?"

"It's a writ, my friend; a writ. You would not tell me the name of your solicitor, so I try personal service instead."

With a beaming smile and a nod of his head, Mr. Rosenbaum swaggered away. In a somewhat bewildered state of mind Mr. Ely stared after him, the paper in his hand.

"It never rains but it pours! Here's two strokes of luck in a single day, and I've only just got out of bed!"

He opened the legal-looking document with which he had been so unexpectedly presented by his generous friend, and glanced at its contents. It was headed "Rosenbaum v. Ely," and, so far as he could judge from his hasty glance, it purported to relate to an action brought by Ruth Rosenbaum against Frederic Ely, to recover damages for breach of promise of marriage.

"Well! This is a pretty go!"

He could scarcely believe his eyes; the damages were laid at thirty thousand pounds! And he had already spent twenty pounds for an engagement-ring!

His first impulse was to tear the paper up and scatter the pieces in the street. His second—which he followed—was to place it in the inner pocket of his coat as a companion to his letter-case.

"Rosenbaum must be a greater fool even than I thought. Thirty thousand pounds! By George! One girl values me at a considerably higher figure than another does."

He found that Mr. Ash was still in his office, and alone; so, without troubling to have himself announced, he marched straight in.

"Hallo, Ely, here again! Anything settled about the date? Or is it something more tangible than love?"

Mr. Ash was engaged with a file of correspondence, from which he looked up at Mr. Ely, with a laugh.

"I have to get through all this before I can put in an appearance in the House. And here's a man who gives me so many minute directions about what he wants to do that I can't for the life of me understand what it is he wants. Why people can't just say 'Buy this,' 'Sell that,' is more than I can tell. But what's the matter? You look quite glum."

"So would you look glum if you had as much cause for looking glum as me."

"I don't know! You've won one of the prettiest girls in England—and one of the nicest little fortunes, too. After that it would take something to make me look glum."

"She's one of the prettiest girls in England."

"There's no mistake about that. Any man might be proud of such a prize. I've been thinking about it all night."

"I've been thinking about it, too."

"And the result is to give you that dyspeptic look? Not flattering to her, eh?"

There was a pause before Mr. Ely answered. With much deliberation he put his hand into his pocket and drew out his letter-case. "I'm sorry you don't think it's flattering." Another pause before he spoke again; then it was with an even more acidulated expression of countenance. "I have received a letter by this morning's post."

"No! From her? She's going it."

"Yes, she is going it, I think."

"That sort of thing's hardly your line, eh?"

"That sort of thing hardly is my line."

"Don't care for love-letters—as a rule?"

"I should like to refer to a dictionary to know what a love-letter is. If this is a love-letter, I prefer a summons."

It was on his tongue to say a writ, but he remembered that he already had one in his pocket, and chose another word.

"Ah, Ely, you must remember that this is a romantic girl. If her language seems too flowery—too kissy-kissy—you must bear in mind that in romantic girls affection is apt to take such shapes. Besides, I should think you'd rather have that than the other kind of thing—I know I would."

"Perhaps, before you pass an opinion on that subject, you'll allow me to read to you the letter I've received."

"Read it! I say! Is that quite fair? Men don't read their love-letters even to their young women's guardians as a rule. Especially the first—I thought that was sacred above the rest."

"Look here, Ash, I'm the mildest-mannered man alive, but you never came nearer having an inkstand at your head than since I've been inside this room."

"Ely! Good gracious, man! What's the matter now?"

"I repeat—perhaps you'll allow me to read to you the letter I've received."

With the same air of excessive deliberation, Mr. Ely opened his letter-case, took from it an envelope, and from it a letter, unfolded the epistle, and looked at Mr. Ash. Mr. Ash did nothing but stare at him.

"This is my first love-letter—the one which you thought was sacred above the rest. I don't know about the rest. This is quite enough for me. You are sure you're listening?"

"I'll take my oath on that."

"'Dear Mr. Ely' (you observe how warmly she begins! Kissy-kissy kind of way, you know), 'just a line with reference to what passed between us yesterday.' (That's a gentle allusion to the trivial fact that on the day before she pledged herself to be my wife. We're getting warm, you see.) 'I have changed my mind.'"

"She has what?"

"She says that she has changed her mind."

"What does she mean by she's changed her mind?"

"Ah, that's what we have to see. It's an obscure allusion which becomes clearer later on; an example of the flowery language in which romantic girls indulge. 'I thought it better to let you know at the earliest possible moment.' (You'll observe that she wastes no time. Perhaps that's another characteristic of the romantic state of mind.) 'It is quite impossible for me to be your wife.'"

"What's that?"

"She says that it's quite impossible for her to be my wife."

"But—good heavens!—I thought you told me she said yes."

"She did say yes."

"But an unhesitating—a final and decisive yes?"

"It was an unhesitating, a final and decisive yes.

"You sent me up a wire!"

"It was agreed between us that I should send you up a wire."

"You talked about having the marriage in a month."

"I did talk, about having the marriage in a month."

"And buying a house and furniture, and all the rest of it."

"Precisely; and all the rest of it."

"And you told me that you had bought a ring."

"That's a fact. I did. I paid twenty pounds for an engagement-ring. It's in my pocket now. That's one of the pleasantest parts of the affair."

113

"Then what the dickens does she mean? Is the girl stark mad? Are you sure the letter comes from her?"

"You shall examine it for yourself in a moment, and then you'll be able to decide. You understand it is the first love-letter I ever had, and therefore sacred above the rest. As for what she means, the explanation comes a little further on—in the next sentence, in fact, Perhaps you will allow me to proceed!"

"Oh, go on! It is plain the girl is mad."

"'The fact is, I am going to marry Mr. Summers instead.'"

"Good—! What—what's that?"

"She says that she's going to marry Mr. Summers instead."

"Instead! Instead of whom?"

"Instead of me."

"Well, I'm—hanged!"

"Yes, that's exactly what I am. And as this is the result of my first love-letter, I don't want to have a second experience of the same kind, you understand."

"Then he's done it after all! What a fool I've been!"

"Well, it does seem that there's a fool somewhere in the case."

"I've done it all!"

"The deuce you have!"

"Do you know this man Summers?"

"Of course I do. Didn't you see I did when I met him here the other day?"

"Do you know what he came for then?"

"How should I? For half a crown, I shouldn't be surprised. He's one of those painter fellows who run up pictures by the yard."

"He came for Lily."

"What the dickens do you mean?"

"I mean exactly what I say. He came to ask my consent to make my ward an offer of his hand."

"What! Before I did?"

"No; directly you had gone."

"But you had given your consent to me!"

"I told him so. He didn't seem to think that it mattered in the least."

"Well, he's a cool hand, upon my Sam!"

"When I told him what I had arranged with you, he wanted to start off for Shanklin there and then. It was with the greatest difficulty that I got him to listen to common sense—I never saw a man in such a state of imbecility. Finally, I agreed that if you failed then he should have his chance."

"But I didn't fail."

"Well, it looks queer."

"Looks queer! Do you want to drive me mad? And I paid twenty pounds for my engagement-ring! Do you think I should buy engagement-rings if I wasn't sure that it was clear? A girl promises to be my wife, and another man comes directly after and eggs her on to break her word! Looks queer! I should think it does, by George! Look here, Ash, if you think I'm going to sit down quietly and stand this sort of thing, you're wrong!"

"Shall I tell you what my own opinion of the matter is?"

"Get it out!"

"The girl's a fool!"

"She's either that or something worse."

"I have only to go down and talk the matter over with her quietly, and you'll see it will be all right."

"You go down! And where do you suppose that I shall be?"

"You leave the matter in my hands, and you'll find that I will make it all right."

"I'll be shot if I will! The girl has promised to be my wife, and if there's any man who's got a right to talk to her it's me. I've had one day out of town; I think I'll spare myself another. You've got a time-table, haven't you? When is there a train?"

Producing a Bradshaw, Mr. Ash plunged into its intricacies.

"It's now eleven. There's a train leaves Waterloo eleven thirty-five. Reaches Shanklin three forty-three. It's too late for that."

"Eleven thirty-five? Is it too late—we'll see. You don't seem to be aware of the fact that at this moment, for all I know, that man's amusing himself with the woman who promised to be my wife. It don't occur to you that there is any necessity for haste. I'm off; you may come or stay, just as you please."

"I'll come—it's a little awkward, but I'll come."

"It is awkward! You'd think it awkward if you were in the pair of shoes that I'm wearing now."

"Half a minute! Just let me speak one word to my managing man."

Mr. Ash called in his clerk. Mr. Ely passed into the street, and engaged a hansom cab. In a remarkably short space of time he was joined by Mr. Ash. Mr. Ely gave instructions to the cabman.

"Waterloo! Main line! And go like blazes!"

And the cab was off.

CHAPTER XI

AN ENCOUNTER IN THE TRAIN

Mr. Ely's last journey from Shanklin up to town had not been exactly of a cheerful kind. Mr. Rosenbaum's appearance on the scene had put a damper on to that. The tale of the six daughters had banished peace from the successful wooer's mind. The journey from town to Shanklin was not exactly pleasant either. Under the best of circumstances Mr. Ely was not the most cheerful of companions. Under existing circumstances he was the most cheerless man alive.

He showed his mettle at the start.

"First-class smoking," Mr. Ash suggested to the guard.

Mr. Ely pulled up short.

"Not for me."

"What do you mean?"

"No smoking carriage for me. I've got enough on my hands already, without having to disinfect myself immediately I arrive."

So they were shown into a non-smoking compartment. Mr. Ash wished his friend at Jericho. The idea of a journey to Portsmouth without the aid of a cigar did not commend itself to him. Besides, he knew that Miss Truscott had liberal-minded notions on the subject of tobacco. But he deemed it prudent to refrain from treading on the tail of the coat which Mr. Ely was obviously trailing on the ground. And he had his revenge!

Just as the train was actually starting there was a cry of "Stop!" Some one came rushing down the platform, the door was opened, and first a lady and then a gentleman were assisted in.

"That was a narrow squeak!" exclaimed the gentleman. Then he turned laughing to the lady: "That's a nice beginning, Mrs. B." The lady laughed at him again. "It's a matter of no importance, but I suppose all our luggage is left behind." He put his head out of the window to see. "No, they're putting it in! In such a style! What a scene of ruin will greet our eyes when we reach the other end."

He drew his head into the compartment and took a survey of his surroundings.

"What, Ash! What, Ely! Here's a go! What brings you two thieves in here? Quite a happy family, my boys."

The gentleman extended one hand to Mr. Ash and the other to Mr. Ely. Mr. Ash laughingly grasped the one which came his way; Mr. Ely acidly declined the other, but the gentleman did not seem to be in the least cast down. He gave Mr. Ely a resounding thwack upon the shoulder, which doubled him up as though he were some lay figure.

"Ely, my boy, you look as though you had been living on sour apples for a week! What's the matter with him, Ash? Been induced to lend his aged mother half a crown? He'll never get over it, you know."

"Mr. Bailey," gasped Mr. Ely, "I'll trouble you not to play your practical jokes on me."

Mr. Bailey laughed. Behind the cover of his paper Mr. Ash laughed too. Mr. Bailey—better known as "Jack" Bailey—was also a member of the "House," and as such known both to Mr. Ely and to Ash. One of those hearty, healthy Englishmen, who having not the slightest reserve themselves have no notion of the existence of such a sense in anybody else. He was Mr. Ely's particular abhorrence. When Mr. Bailey had done laughing, he turned to the lady who accompanied him. She was a feminine repetition of himself: a tall, strapping, buxom wench, with bright black eyes and bright red cheeks; the very embodiment of health and strength; the sort of damsel who is in her element on the tennis-lawn or on the river, or doing four-and-twenty dances off the reel.

"Who do you think that is?"

The lady laughed.

"Jack! shut up," she said.

"Just hark at her! We've not been married an hour, and she's beginning to order me about already! Allow me to introduce you to my wife, Mrs. Bailey —Miss Williamson that was. Married this morning in the Church of St. Michael and All Angels, six bridesmaids, and such a wedding-cake! Only we couldn't stop to eat this wedding-cake, we had to catch the train!"

Mr. and Mrs. Bailey laughed again. Mr. Ash laughed too. But Mr. Ely—he turned green. Mr. Ash raised his hat and bowed to the lady.

"Allow me to offer you my congratulations, Mrs. Bailey. Am I justified in supposing that you are starting on your honeymoon?"

"Justified! I should think you are!" Seating himself, Mr. Bailey slipped his arm about the lady's waist. "I say, Bess, it's lucky we've fallen among men I know. I should have had to apologise for kissing you in front of strangers."

He kissed her then. But the lady only laughed.

"You know Jack," she explained. "Every one knows Jack! He has a way of his own."

"I should think I have got a way of my own!" cried the gentleman referred to. And he slipped the lady on to his knee. "I wouldn't give a button for the man who hadn't; eh, Ely, what do you say? I say, Ely, why don't you go in for something in this line?"

And he nodded towards his wife.

"I'm afraid I do not understand you."

"He says he doesn't understand me, Bess. Isn't that a funny man?"

"Are you not married, Mr. Ely?" inquired the bride of an hour.

"I have not that happiness."

For the life of him Mr. Ash could not have resisted the chance which offered.

"But he's going to be—he's engaged," he said.

Mr. Ely turned the colour of a boiled beetroot. But Mr. and Mrs. Bailey quite mistook the reason. It was not because he was shy; it was because the exigencies of civilisation debarred him from cutting Mr. Ash's throat.

"I wish you joy!" exclaimed the gentleman.

"When's it going to be!" chimed in the lady.

"I'll be best man!"

"If you promise to send me a piece of the cake I'll let you have a piece of mine."

Mr. Bailey turned to his wife.

"To look at him you wouldn't think he was engaged, now, would you?"

"Why? Is there anything funny about the looks of a man when he's engaged?"

"Funny! I should think there is! Ely, what do you think? Don't you feel funny? You ought to if you don't."

"May I inquire, Mr. Bailey, what you mean?"

There was such a savage tone in Mr. Ely's voice that even the not quick-witted Mr. Bailey was struck by it.

"Hallo! What's up now? I say, Ash, you ought to tip a fellow the wink when a man's had an unfortunate misunderstanding with his best girl."

"Mr. Bailey—I beg Mrs. Bailey's pardon,—but I suppose that in the presence of a lady you take it for granted that you may permit yourself the utmost license of speech."

Mr. Bailey whistled, Mrs. Bailey laughed, then looked out of the window with a look of innocent surprise—that look of innocent surprise which means so much. Mr. Bailey nudged his wife with his elbow.

"Beautiful scenery, isn't it?"

They were then passing a long, level stretch of what seemed turnip-fields. Mrs. Bailey laughed again.

"Ah, it's a serious thing to have a misunderstanding with your best girl!"

Mrs. Bailey laughed again.

"It's all very well to laugh, but I've had more than one, and nobody knows what it feels like who hasn't gone through it all. Poor chap, no wonder he feels down!"

"Mr. Ely," explained the lady, "never you mind Jack, it's a way he's got; he will always have his joke." Then she showed the tact for which women are so famous. "I hope that there really has been no misunderstanding with—with the lady?"

"S—sh!—Bess!—For shame!—I'm surprised at you! I wouldn't have asked such a question, not for a thousand pounds!"

"Mr. Bailey, if the worst comes to the worst, I feel quite convinced that you will be able to provide Mrs. Bailey with an excellent establishment by becoming a professional buffoon."

This was Mr. Ely's final word. The train just then drew up at Guildford. Mr. Bailey rose with the air of a martyr.

"I'm afraid, my dear Bess, we must really tear ourselves away. We ought to find a separate compartment. Our friends are most anxious to smoke, and the presence of a lady prevents them, you know."

When the pair were gone, Mr. Ely turned upon Mr. Ash with something that was very much like a snarl.

"I have to thank you for that."

"For what? What do you mean?"

"You know very well what I mean. For that clown's impertinence—great, lumbering buffoon!"

"Good gracious, Ely, you don't seem to be in the pleasantest of moods. What did I tell him? I only said you were engaged. What harm is there in that? I don't know what good you expect to come from keeping it hidden from the world."

Mr. Ely turned the matter over in his mind. He gnashed his teeth, not figuratively, but very literally indeed.

"By George, I'll make her marry me, or I'll know the reason why!"

"One way to that desirable consummation is to compromise the lady's name. Advertise the fact that she has promised to be your wife."

"If I thought that, I'd stick it up on every dead wall in town."

"Let's try milder means at first. Leave more vigorous measures to a little later on. Unless I'm much mistaken, you'll find the milder means will serve. There's a little misunderstanding, that is all."

"Little misunderstanding you call it, do you? I should like to know what you call a big one, then."

If they did not actually come to blows they did more than one little bit of figurative sparring on the way. Mr. Ash found it best to keep quite still. Directly he opened his mouth Mr. Ely showed an amazing disposition to snap at his nose. For instance, once when the train stopped at a station—

"This is Rowland's Castle, isn't it?"

"No, it isn't Rowland's Castle. I should like to know what on earth makes you think it's Rowland's Castle. I wonder you don't say it's Colney Hatch."

Mr. Ash gazed mildly at his friend, and subsided into his paper. He felt that with things as they were conversation might be labelled "dangerous."

CHAPTER XII

THE RIVALS—NEW VERSION

When they reached Shanklin, Mr. Ely was shown into the drawing-room, while Mr. Ash disappeared upstairs.

"You wait in there," suggested Mr. Ash; "there's a word or two I want to say to the old lady. I want to get to the bottom of the thing, because it's quite possible we've come on a wild goose chase after all. You wait half a minute, and I'll see Miss Lily's sent to you. I shouldn't be at all surprised to see her come flying headlong into your arms. Then you'll find out that it's almost worth while to fall out for the sake of the reconciliation."

Left alone in the drawing-room, Mr. Ely was not by any means so sure. He was inclined to be sceptical as to the young lady's flying leap into his arms. And as to falling out for the sake of the reconciliation—well, there might be something, perhaps, in that, but he would like to have felt as sure about the reconciliation as he did about the falling out.

He seated himself on an ottoman, thrust his hands into his trousers pockets, and stared at his patent toes. A minute passed, more than a minute, more than five minutes, indeed, still he was left alone. He looked at his watch. Ten minutes had elapsed since he entered the room.

"This is a pretty state of things; ten living minutes have I sat stewing here! And Ash said that in less than half a minute he wouldn't be surprised to see her in my arms. It looks like it!"

He got up and surveyed the apartment.

"I wonder where she is? And where the other fellow is? That's the man to whom I ought to apply for information. I lay my hat that she's done some bounding into his arms since yesterday. That's a pleasant thought to think about the woman who's promised to be your wife!"

Mr. Ely disconsolately paced the room.

"And to think that I paid twenty pounds for an engagement-ring! And I might have forked up forty-five! That's what gets at me! And I've got Rosenbaum's writ in my coat pocket. Damages laid at thirty thousand pounds! Oh, lor! This is a nice day's work I've done!"

Pausing before the fireplace he leaned his elbow on the mantelshelf, and his head upon his hand, and groaned.

"Excuse me, but can you tell me where Miss Truscott is?" There was a voice behind him. Mr. Ely turned.

"Hallo, Ely! I had no idea that it was you! How are you, dear old man?"

Mr. Ely turned—metaphorically—into a pillar of ice. Into a pillar of red-hot ice, if we may confound our metaphors. For while his exterior demeanour was several degrees below zero, his interior economy left boiling point at the post.

A gentleman had strolled into the room through the opened window—Mr. William Summers. Mr. William Summers as large as life, and larger. There were no signs of guilt upon his countenance; certainly there were none in his bearing. He held a soft crush hat in one hand, the other he held out to Mr. Ely.

"Well, I'm—hanged!"

"I say, Ely, what's the row?"

Speechless with indignation, Mr. Ely turned and strode towards the door. When he reached it he paused, and turning again, he gazed at the intruder. The intruder did not seem to be at all abashed.

"That's the way they used to do it at the Coburg. Exit vanquished vice."

"Sir!"

"That's a little Coburg, too. They used to roll their r's."

Mr. Summers tugged at his beard. Retracing his steps, Mr. Ely strode on until he was in a measurable distance of Mr. Summers's nose.

"Understand this once for all: you are a perfect stranger, sir, to me."

"That's all right; I thought I was. Excuse one stranger speaking to another, but could you tell me where Miss Truscott is?"

Mr. Ely gasped. "This—this beats anything I ever heard of! Mr. Summers!"

"That's right, Ely, I'm awake. Wire in and lay me flat; I sha'n't mind a bit."

"In all this there may be something funny, sir, which commends it to your mind—if you have a mind—but I see nothing comic in desecrating nature's most sacred ties and in corrupting the innocence of youth."

"More don't I, Ely; not the way you put it—and I couldn't put it better if I tried."

"Are you aware that Miss Truscott has promised to be my wife?"

"Ah, that was a mistake!"

"A mistake! What the devil do you mean?"

"You see, Ely, I've been in love with her a good twelve months—aye, that and more. I fell in love with her the first moment she came across my path."

"What the dickens do I care if you've been in love with her twelve years? More shame you! Do you consider that a justification to the scoundrel who betrays another fellow's wife?"

"In love with her in a sense you do not understand—in love with her with my whole life."

"What on earth has that to do with me?"

"I have lived for her, and worked, and hoped, and dreamed, until she has grown to be the centre of my being. Does she mean all that to you?"

"What business have you to ask me such a question? When you have ruined Mrs. Jones do you put a similar inquiry to Jones? I should think Jones would feel that you were a logical sort of person if you did."

"Ah, but here she is not your wife."

"But she's going to be!"

"As I live she never will."

"Hang it, sir; don't I tell you that she promised?"

"And don't I tell you that was a mistake. If you will keep cool I will give you an explanation. If you decline to listen to an explanation, you must be content to realise the fact."

"Look here, Mr. Summers, you are a sort of man with whom I have had very little to do—"

"My misfortune—not your fault."

"But I suppose you have some idea of common decency, if you have none of honour—"

"I hope I have."

"And I ask you if you think it's decent, directly a woman has promised a man to be his wife, to go behind his back and induce the woman to dishonour herself and him?"

"But that is not what I have done."

"It is what you have done. One day Miss Truscott promises to be my wife, the next—directly my back is turned—you come and persuade her to be false to herself and me."

"My good Ely, there is one factor you are omitting from your calculations, and that is—love."

"Which with you stands higher—love or honesty?"

"Oh, they both go hand-in-hand. Would it have been honest for her to have married you when she loved me?"

"Pooh! Stuff and nonsense! I never heard such impudence! What the dickens do you mean by saying that the woman who has promised to be my wife loves you?"

"You perceive, it is from that that I saved you—that curse of all existence, that canker which eats into the very root of life—a loveless marriage. But there are not many signs of gratitude, that I can see."

And Mr. Summers sighed. Mr. Ely gasped.

"Look here, Mr. Summers, I am not a fighting man."

"No?"

"But if I were—!"

"Yes. If you were? Go on!"

"By George, sir, if I were—!" At this moment Mr. Ash entered the room. "I'm sorry, Ash, that you have come. You've interrupted the most agreeable interview that I ever had in all my life."

"I'm surprised, Mr. Summers, after what has passed, to see you here."

"Why? I assure you I'm not at all surprised at seeing you."

Rising, Mr. Summers held out his hand. But Mr. Ash declined to see it.

"Oh, take his hand! For goodness' sake take his hand! Shake it off his wrist! Don't let him suppose that you're not delighted to have the pleasure."

"Our friend Ely—"

"Your friend Ely! What the dickens, sir, do you mean by calling me your friend?"

Very red in the face, Mr. Ely struck an attitude in front of Mr. Summers which was probably intended to express ferocity. Mr. Summers tugged at his beard, and smiled. Mr. Ash interposed.

"I can hardly think, Mr. Summers, that it is necessary for me to suggest that your presence is not required here."

"My dear fellow, I am only waiting to obtain a little information."

"What information can you possibly expect to receive?"

"I only want to know where Miss Truscott is."

"Yes, that's all! That's all he wants to know! A more modest request I never heard! He only wants to know where my wife is!"

"Excuse me, Ely, but Miss Truscott is not your wife!"

"But she's going to be!"

"That she will never be!"

"Hang it, sir!" Mr. Ely rushed forward. But again Mr. Ash thought it advisable to interpose.

"Mr. Summers, be so kind as to leave this house."

"Oh, don't turn him out! For goodness' sake don't turn him out! Pray tell him where the lady is! And also acquaint him with the situation of the spoons! And entreat him, next time he calls, to bring his burglar friends, and other relatives."

Mr. Ash endeavoured to pacify his friend. But the attempt was vain. Mr. Ely's blood was up. His wrongs were more than he could bear.

"My dear Ely, I beg that you will not pay the slightest attention to this— gentleman."

"Attention! Not me! I'm not paying the attention! It's he! And to my young woman, by the Lord!"

Still tugging at his beard, Mr. Summers laughed and turned away.

"I'm sorry you cannot give me the information I require. And you really are inhospitable, Ash, you really are. But never mind, I'll have my revenge! When you come to see me I'll not show you the door; nor Ely, if he'll condescend to call."

He had reached the window when the door opened, and Mrs. Clive appeared.

"Ah, here is Mrs. Clive! I am sure that Mrs. Clive will take pity on a man, especially a man in the forlorn situation which I am. May I ask if you can tell me where I am likely to find Miss Truscott?"

"Mr. Summers!"

Mrs. Clive's attitude was a study. It was as though all the pokers in England were down her back. But Mr. Summers did not show any sign of discomposure.

"Surely you will not be hard upon a man, especially upon a man in love. Consider our position. I seek Lily, she seeks me. Life's summer-time is short. You would not have us waste its sweetness?"

"Mr. Summers, I am more amazed than I can say."

"Oh, don't be amazed! For goodness' sake don't be amazed! And don't be hard upon a man—especially upon a man in love! Consider his position, and don't waste the sweetness of life's summer-time—oh, don't, for gracious' sake!" Mr. Ely pulled up his shirt-collar and "shot" his cuffs. "I reckon I'm spending one of the pleasantest half hours I ever had in all my life."

"Mrs. Clive, will you not listen to the all-conquering voice, the voice of love?"

"Mr. Summers, I must decline to listen to another word. And I am amazed to think that you should attempt to address me at all, especially as I have given you to understand that our acquaintance, sir, had ceased."

"Ceased! And I am going to marry your niece! Could you so divide the family? She who loves you so! And whom, for her sweet sake and Pompey's, I love too?"

"Well, this—this does beat cock-fighting! That allusion to Pompey was one of the most touching things I've heard. And he is going to marry your niece, so you and I, Ash, had better go back to town."

And again Mr. Ely's collar and cuffs came into play. Mr. Ash advanced.

"Mr. Summers, I have already requested you to go. You can scarcely wish us to use force."

"No, not force—not that. If it must be then—goodbye! After all, parting is such sweet sorrow. Goodbye, Mrs. Clive, you will weep for me when I am gone. Ta-ta, Ely, we shall meet at Philippi—I leave you—yes, you three!— perchance to wrangle, in very truth thinking angry thoughts—in such an air of discord, too! While I—I go under the shadow of the trees, where love lies dreaming—and waiting perhaps for me. If I meet Miss Truscott, Ely—and I shall under the trysting tree—I will tell her that if you had been a fighting man you certainly would have murdered me."

CHAPTER XIII

THE LOVER GREETS THE LADY

There was a pause when he had gone.

Mrs. Clive, the very essence of dignified disapprobation, stood in the centre of the room. Mr. Ash, a little flustered, was near the window, first gazing through it in the direction which Mr. Summers had taken, and then, a little dubiously, out of the corners of his eyes at his indignant friend. Mr. Ely's hands were in his trouser pockets, his legs were wide apart his countenance was red. He seemed to be in a very dissatisfied frame of mind indeed.

It was he who broke the silence.

"You see, Ash, it was a wild goose chase we came upon! That man looks like it, by George!"

"My dear fellow, I hope you will not pay the slightest attention to what that person says. He is the kind of man who will say anything. I assure you there is not the slightest occasion for you to feel concerned."

From Mr. Ash's manner it almost seemed as though he desired to convey a greater feeling of assurance that he quite felt himself. He cast several glances in the direction of Mrs. Clive, as though seeking for support.

"It depends upon what you call the 'slightest occasion' for concern," retorted Mr. Ely drily. "When a man tells you that he is going to marry the girl who has promised to be your wife, and that he is going to meet her underneath the trysting tree—where love lies dreaming, he said, by gad!— some people would think that there was some reason to feel concerned!"

Mr. Ash smiled and rubbed his hands, and fidgeted upon his feet, and looked at Mrs. Clive. He seemed to find some difficulty in finding something suitable to say. But Mrs. Clive came nobly to his rescue.

She advanced to Mr. Ely with a smiling countenance and an outstretched hand.

"Good afternoon, Mr. Ely; you have not spoken to me yet. I am pleased to have you back with us so soon."

Mr. Ely seemed in two minds at first as to whether he should take her hand. Then he just touched it with his own.

"Good afternoon, ma'am! If you're pleased, I'm sure I am—though I must say your pleasure's easily found."

But the old lady was not to be so easily put down. Her cue seemed to be to assume unconsciousness of there being anything unpleasant in the air.

"The pleasure of your visit is heightened by its unexpectedness. Lily has been working all the morning in her room upstairs—you have no idea how industrious she is."

Mr. Ely looked at her suspiciously, as though he doubted if she were a strict exponent of the truth.

"I thought he said that he was going to meet her underneath the trysting tree!"

The old lady smiled a superior smile.

"You really must not believe such nonsense as that. I assure you it is the greatest presumption upon his part."

"It would require a good deal of assurance to make me believe that it was not."

"Lily will be with us directly. Young ladies cannot rush into a gentleman's presence quite at a moment's notice, you know."

"I beg that Miss Truscott will take her time!"

Mr. Ely marched to the other end of the room, and stood looking in rather too obvious admiration at an engraving after Landseer which hung upon the wall. Mrs. Clive, a little disconcerted, was left to make conversation with Mr. Ash. But Mr. Ash was in a distinctly uneasy frame of mind.

"I suppose," he said in a whisper to the lady, keeping one eye fixed on Mr. Ely all the time, "I suppose she'll come?"

"My dear Mr. Ash, what do you mean?"

The lady's modulated tones betrayed the most intense surprise. Mr. Ash coughed. His manner was apologetic. But without volunteering an explanation he sauntered off towards Mr. Ely. He had hardly taken a step when the door opened and Miss Truscott appeared. The young lady's entrance, in its way, was perfect. She was so extremely at her ease. She stood at the door a moment, and then advanced with outstretched hands and the sweetest smile to Mr. Ash. She did not seem to notice Mr. Ely. He, on his part, continued to admire the engraving.

"Guardian! How kind of you to take me by surprise like this!"

Mr. Ash took the two hands she offered and looked at her. Certainly this was a woman whom no man need be ashamed to call his wife. Tall above the average of her sex, yet her figure was exquisitely feminine—she bore herself with the daintiest grace. She was dressed in white from head to foot; a silver belt went round her waist; in the belt were some red roses; there was another rosebud in the bosom of her dress. As Mr. Ash held her two soft, white hands in his he involuntarily glanced in the direction of the dapper little gentleman who was continuing to examine the engraving which hung upon the wall. Even if they made a match of it they would scarcely make a pair, these two.

"What have you to say for yourself?" asked the lady, seeing that he was still. "Do you know how long it is since you came to look upon my face? Does your conscience not reproach you, sir? I suppose it is the Juggernaut of commerce which has kept you so long away?"

Mr. Ash smiled, and pressed her hands. Possibly the source from which she drew the reference to the Juggernaut of commerce was still fresh in his mind, for there was something a little uneasy in his smile.

"I think you will allow that I have atoned for my misconduct when you perceive whom I have brought as my companion."

Mr. Ash motioned towards Mr. Ely with his now disengaged hand. Miss Truscott turned with her most innocent air. When she perceived the little gentleman, her countenance was illumined with a seraphic smile.

"Mr. Ely! Who would have thought of seeing you? This is a compliment! To be able to tear yourself away again so quickly from your Noras and Doras, and bulls and bears."

Mr. Ely ceased to examine the engraving. Turning, he pulled his spotless white waistcoat down into its place, and then thrust his thumbs into the armholes. He looked the lady in the face.

"I knew you would be surprised," he said.

"Surprised! Surprised is not the word!" Then she turned again to Mr. Ash. "Guardian, would you like to look at the garden? You have no idea how beautiful it is."

Mr. Ash cleared his throat. He felt that this was a defiance, that in these seemingly innocent words the gage of challenge was thrown down. Miss Truscott was quite aware that he had not come down to look at the garden. He looked at Mr. Ely, but that gentleman kept his eyes fixed upon his faithless fair one with a sort of glare. He looked at Mrs. Clive, but there were no signs that help was likely to come from there. The stockbroker felt that it was incumbent upon him to come to the point.

"My dear Lily, I shall be delighted to see the garden—delighted—by and by!" This interpolation was necessary because the young lady sailed towards the window as though she wished to fly into the garden on the wings of the wind. "Before I can give myself that pleasure, there is one little point which I should like to have cleared up."

Miss Truscott, brought to a standstill, looked down at the toe of the little shoe with which she was tapping the floor.

"Yes, guardian. What is that?"

Nothing could be better—in its way—than the air of shy, sweet modesty with which she asked the question. But Mr. Ash felt that it was a little disconcerting all the same.

"It's—eh!—rather a delicate point for an old—and crusty—bachelor like me to handle."

Mr. Ash said this with an air of forced joviality which was anything but jovial. His gruesome effort to be cheerful seemed to strike Miss Truscott, for she gave him a quick, penetrating glance which took him considerably aback.

"Guardian! Aren't you well?"

"Well? God bless the girl, yes! What do you mean?"

Back went the eyes to the toe, which again began tapping the floor. "I didn't know."

Mr. Ash pulled himself together. He made another effort, and began again. He was not a man who was deficient in tact as a rule, but he was conscious that his was a position in which even something more than tact might be required. Joining the tips of his fingers, he balanced himself upon his toes and heels, assuming what he intended to be a judicial attitude.

"My dear Lily, you are quite aware that you have reached an age at which it is no longer possible to treat you as a girl."

"Would you treat me as an old woman, then?"

This was disconcerting; even more disconcerting was the glance with which it was accompanied. Mr. Ash—who had the sense of humour which Mr. Ely lacked—was quite aware that the young lady was laughing in her sleeve, and he had very clearly in his mind the memory of previous occasions on which the young lady had beaten him with weapons against which none of his were of the least avail. Still, he stuck to his guns. Was not Mr. Ely looking on? And Mrs. Clive?

"I would treat you as a person who has arrived at years of discretion, who

is conscious of the meaning of the words which she may use. One moment!"
For Miss Truscott murmured something about her not being yet twenty-one,
and he felt that interruption might be fatal. "Lily, you are at least aware of
what a promise means."

The young lady sighed.

"It depends," she said.

"Depends!—depends on what?"

She looked up. Feeling that it would be impossible for him to preserve his
gravity and yet meet the wicked light which he knew was in her eyes, Mr.
Ash's glance in turn sought refuge on the ground.

"Supposing," she explained, "when you were suffering from an attack of
indigestion you promised a friend to cut your throat—you know what one is
inclined to promise when one does feel ill. Would you feel constrained to
carry out your promise when you found that a dose of somebody's medicine
had brought you round?"

Mr. Ash was still. Mrs. Clive took up the parable instead.

"Lily! I'm amazed at you!"

"My dear aunt, why are you amazed?"

"I never thought a niece of mine could have acted so."

Miss Truscott sighed.

"It seems to me that of late I'm always doing wrong. I don't know how it
is. I think I had better go into the garden all alone."

She gave a half-step towards the window. Mr. Ash cleared his throat with
rather a suspicious "hem!"

"It won't do, Lily. I know your genius for turning serious questions upside
down, but I ask you to put it to your conscience if, on the present occasion,
that is fair. A matter which affects the lives of a man and of a woman ought to
be approached with gravity at least."

"Is the woman me?" She looked at him out of the corners of her eyes.
"Oughtn't that to be—Is the woman I?" Then she broke into a smile. "What
can you expect when even the elementary rules of grammar are not there?"

So far Mr. Ely had kept a judicious, if not a judicial, silence. But when he
saw that Miss Truscott was smiling at Mr. Ash, and more than suspected that
Mr. Ash was smiling back at her, he felt that it was time for him to speak.

"If you will allow me, Ash, I'll manage this myself."

"Delighted, my dear fellow, I am sure!"

"I fancy I am the person principally concerned."

"Quite so, quite so!"

"If you will leave me alone with Miss Truscott, I've no doubt that in a few minutes we shall understand each other very well indeed."

"I'm sure you will! I feel quite sure you will!"

Mr. Ash's tone was cheerful—Mr. Ely felt that it was even exasperatingly cheerful. Advancing, he laid his hand upon his ward's well-rounded arm.

"Mind you behave yourself," he told her. Then he left the room.

"Lily," said Mrs. Clive, when Mr. Ash had gone, "I trust you will do credit to the precepts which I have so constantly, and I hope conscientiously, endeavoured to instil into your mind, and that I shall not have cause to blush for my own sister's child."

Then Mrs. Clive went after Mr. Ash, and the two were left alone.

CHAPTER XIV

THE LADY ENDEAVOURS TO EXPLAIN

"Sounds like the last words of a funeral sermon," muttered Mr. Ely, directly the door was closed.

"It does sound a little that way, doesn't it?"

Then the two were still.

Mr. Ely took up the position in front of the fireplace which had been occupied by Mr. Ash; Miss Truscott seated herself by a five-o'clock tea-table, and pensively regarded so much of her toes as she permitted to peep from under the hem of her dress. A considerable pause ensued. Possibly Mr. Ely was endeavouring to find words with which to clothe his thoughts.

"This is like a Quaker's meeting," murmured the lady.

Mr. Ely started. But he checked the retort which rose to his lips, and continued his reflections. At last he spoke. The words issued from his lips with excessive deliberation, as though he weighed each one to be quite sure it was of proper weight.

"Miss Truscott, the exigencies of modern civilisation compel from man a chivalrous attitude towards the weaker sex."

She looked up at the first sound of his voice—and he immediately wished she would look down again.

"But there are occasions on which chivalry should give place to even higher things."

He certainly wished she would look down again. Her countenance was perfectly grave, but he had a horrid suspicion that there was laughter in her eyes. She murmured something to herself.

"What was that you said?" he asked, with a sudden departure from his air of ceremonious state.

"Nothing."

She looked down—and smiled. Mr. Ely felt that he was growing warm. He was not a man easily put out of countenance as a rule, but this young lady had an effect upon him which was quite unprecedented. He changed his method of attack, and from excessive deliberation passed to excessive haste.

"Miss Truscott, I am a plain business man."

"You are."

"The day before yesterday I asked you to be my wife."

"You did."

"You said you would."

"And immediately afterwards I changed my mind." She said this with her sweetest smile.

"Changed your mind! What do you mean? Do you know I spent twenty pounds on an engagement-ring?" Mr. Ely produced a little leather case from his waistcoat pocket, and from the case a ring. "Do you see that? Do you know I paid twenty pounds for that? And it might have cost me forty-five."

Taking the ring, Miss Truscott slipped it on her long, slender finger.

"What a pretty ring! How well it fits me, too. I'll buy it from you if you'll let me have it cheap."

Mr. Ely was for a moment speechless.

"Cheap! Do you think I buy engagement-rings to sell them at a profit, then?"

"I don't know. You say you are a business man."

"Say I'm a business man! I should have to be a very funny business man if I did that kind of thing."

Taking off the ring, Miss Truscott put it back into the case.

"Never mind, Mr. Ely; as a business man you know that a good investment is never thrown away. If you don't meet with a good offer for it at once it is sure to come in by and by. If you go on asking girls to marry you, possibly in time you will light on one who will not change her mind."

"Miss Truscott, I don't think you quite know what sort of man I am."

"You say you are a business man."

"But, excuse me, you don't seem to know what a business man is either. A business man is a man who sticks to his own bargains, and expects other people to stick to theirs."

"Is he, indeed. How very interesting!"

"You promised to be my wife."

"Always supposing that I did not change my mind."

"Always supposing nothing of the kind. There was no sort of supposition even hinted at. It was as plain and unequivocal a promise as was ever made by A to B."

"Don't you see, Mr. Ely, that you're placing me in a delicate position?"

"In what sort of a position do you think you're placing me?"

"Would you have me marry you—now?"

"By George, I would!"

Rising from her seat, Miss Truscott placed her two hands behind her back —in the manner in which the children do at school–and looked him boldly in the face.

"When I love another man?—when my whole heart only beats for him?— when, in a sense which you shall never understand, I am his, and he is mine?"

Mr. Ely fidgeted beneath the clear scrutiny of her wide-open eyes.

"Look here, Miss Truscott, I've told you already that I am not a man of sentiment."

"Do you call this a question of sentiment? Would you marry a woman who frankly tells you that she loathes you, and that she yearns for another man?"

"Loathes me, by gad! Nice thing, by George! Look here, Miss Truscott, you promised to be my wife—"

Mr. Ely was accentuating his words by striking together the palms of his hands, but Miss Truscott cut him short.

"Really, Mr. Ely, you are like a child. You indulge in the vainest repetitions. I promised fiddlesticks, for all I know! I don't intend to marry you, so there's an end of it."

"Don't you? We shall see!"

"We certainly shall see!"

"Miss Truscott, if you decline to fulfil the promise which you made to me —according to your own confession—I go straight from here to my solicitor and instruct him to immediately commence an action against you for breach of promise of marriage. You will find that even a woman is not allowed to play fast-and-loose exactly as she pleases."

"You threaten me! You dare to threaten me! Now I see the business man, indeed! It is damages you want to mend your broken heart—the money, not the wife. How foolish I was not to understand all that before! Can we not compromise the case, we principals? Why should all the plunder go into the lawyer's hands? Let me beg your acceptance of a ten-pound note."

Miss Truscott took out her purse.

"Ten pounds!" Mr. Ely remembered the writ which he had in the pocket of his coat. "I'll get thirty thousand pounds at least!"

"Thirty thousand pounds! What a sum am I not valued at! I am afraid, Mr. Ely, that I am not able to treat with you when you speak of such noble figures as that. You see, at present, my guardian has the charge of my pecuniary affairs. But I beg you to believe that I am glad to learn that you can find compensation even in the prospect of such a sum as that. I had feared that your wounded affections were incurable."

"Compensation! Oh, yes, I'll find compensation fast enough! And you shall find it too! That letter of yours shall be produced in court. You shall have as first rate an advertisement as ever yet a woman had. I'll give Summers cause to be proud of his wife."

"I am so pleased to hear you speak like that, because, of course, I hope he always will be proud of me, you know. I hope you will not put it down to my insufferable conceit, but I don't think he's ashamed of me, as yet. But it is quite a relief to my mind to think that we are agreed. For we are agreed, are we not?"

"Agreed! On what?"

"On the principle of compensation."

"Oh, yes, there's no doubt that we agree on that—as you will see directly I get back to town."

"That is most gratifying, isn't it? As we do agree now, won't you take my hand?" Before he knew it she had her hand in his. She was looking at him with laughter lighting all her face. "I knew that we should understand each other after all."

And while they still stood there hand in hand, looking at each other—but with such different expressions on their faces—the door opened and Mr. Ash came in.

CHAPTER XV

THE LADY EXPLAINS STILL FURTHER

"When a woman says she will, she will!
You may depend on't!
And when she says she won't, she won't!
And there's an end on't!"

"I knew you would! I knew you had only got to get together to understand each other perfectly."

This was what Mr. Ash said as he entered the room. He had caught Miss Truscott's words, but misapplied their meaning. He advanced towards Mr. Ely with beaming countenance.

"I congratulate you, Ely; I do with all my heart. Who was right about the little misunderstanding, now? Did I not tell you that there was a romantic side about the feminine character with which you were unacquainted, a sort of airy nothing which is a source of continual perplexity to the most experienced man. And wasn't it worth it all for the sake of the reconciliation at the end?"

Mr. Ely gasped.

"This—this is the final straw!"

"Ah, my boy, I know more about a woman than you. We old bachelors are not quite blind, after all."

It was with difficulty that Mr. Ely obtained sufficient self-control to enable him to speak.

"Do I understand that you are offering me your congratulations?"

"Certainly! I congratulate you with all my heart, my boy."

Mr. Ash held out his hand. Mr. Ely ignored it. He did more. He looked as though he would have liked to have spurned it from him. He eyed Mr. Ash with withering scorn.

"I'm a fit subject for congratulations. I'm the happiest man alive. I suppose there's no man in England who has more cause to bless his stars than I have."

"I am so glad to hear it, Mr. Ely, I cannot tell."

Mr. Ely started as though he had been shot. Mrs. Clive had, in her turn, made her appearance on the scene. She, too, had overheard his words. She came sailing across the room all smiles and condescension.

"I knew my niece, you see. Who should know her if not I? The girl has been to me as my own child. What I learnt at my mother's knees I, in my turn, have taught to her—what she is she owes to me. Receive my sincerest congratulations, Mr. Ely, upon this fortunate event."

Mr. Ely stared at the old lady as though his eyes were starting from his head. It was only after an interval that his thoughts were able to find expression in speech.

"I don't know if all the world has lost its mental equilibrium, or if it's only I! What she is she owes to you? I don't know that I should like to be owed a debt like that, by George! You have taught her what you yourself learnt at your mother's knee? You must have learnt some funny things! And as for your congratulations—as for your congratulations, madam"—Mr. Ely settled his waistcoat in its place—"I don't know if a deliberate insult is intended, but in any case you may postpone your congratulations to a future date."

Mr. Ash looked surprised, Mrs. Clive bewildered. But Miss Truscott laughed—the most musical of little laughs.

"You see, my good people, although you are all of you older than I, there is not one of you who understands."

"That's one consolation," said Mr. Ely, "at any rate."

Miss Truscott, without heeding him, went on, to Mr. Ash's and Mrs. Clive's increasing bewilderment—

"One would really think that love was quite a new creation—you seem never to have heard of it before! You see, guardian"—she turned with an air of the most bewitching frankness to Mr. Ash—"when your letter came I was more than twelve months gone in love. I think that love must be a sort of disease which has to run its course through different stages. I was in the stage of dark despair. At that moment I would have married Pompey had he asked me—I looked on Mr. Ely just as I would have looked on Pompey, you understand."

"Flattering, upon my word!" Mr. Ely was just able to articulate.

But Miss Truscott only looked at him and laughed.

"But the morning after, that stage had passed away, and with it all the things which appertained to it had gone—whether you call it Pompey or Mr. Ely, it is just the same, those things had gone—I was sane again, in my right mind. Love claimed me on that day, and, of course when love claimed me I was his. For to think"—she bore herself quite straight, with her head a little back, so that, in some strange way, she seemed to have grown in stature before their very eyes—"for to think that this to me means love"—she motioned to Mr. Ely with her hand—"this little gentleman of stocks and shares—it is the most foolish thing that ever yet I heard. None knows better than this gentleman himself that love is just the thing he does not even care to understand; and to me, love, with the eternity of meaning the little word conveys, is all the world."

She favoured Mr. Ely with her most sweeping curtsey, the sweetest mockery of laughter in her eyes.

"Mr. Ely, I wish you, sir, good day. For the engagement-ring which cost you twenty pounds I hope that you will find a wearer soon."

She went to the window, and stood just outside, with her finger on her lips.

"One word in confidence. Next time you ask a girl to be your wife, do not insist upon it as your chiefest qualification for the married state that you are indeed a business man!"

She passed down the steps, and across the lawn, and went away; and directly she was out of sight they heard her voice upraised in a burst of joyous song.

CHAPTER XVI

THUNDER IN THE AIR

There was silence in the room—an awkward silence. For some moments nobody seemed to think that there was anything left to say. It was noticeable that neither of the trio seemed to care to look the other in the face. Mr. Ely stood with his hands thrust to the extremest depths of his trouser pockets, staring moodily, not to say savagely, at the window through which Miss Truscott had disappeared. Mr. Ash stroked his chin with something of an embarrassed air—he did not seem to know where to rest his eyes. From the expression of her countenance, and from her bearing altogether, Mrs. Clive seemed to have had the faculty of speech knocked out of her.

As perhaps was natural, Mr. Ely was the first who found his tongue. He pointed his words by looking at Mrs. Clive out of the corners of his eyes.

"That's a nice way in which to bring up a girl!"

His tone was distinctly venomous. Mr. Ash continued to stroke his chin.

"It does seem," he hazarded, in a sort of deprecatory undertone, "it does seem as though she had imbibed some curious ideas."

"That's the sort of girl to do anybody credit."

"I confess," said Mr. Ash with a little cough, as though he wished to apologise for his confession, "I confess that I am surprised."

Mrs. Clive, blissfully unconscious that it could enter into anybody's philosophy to think of attacking her, remained sublimely statuesque.

"I say, without the slightest hesitation, that the person who is responsible for the education of that young woman has committed a crime against society."

Mr. Ely turned on Mrs. Clive with something that was very like a snarl. The old lady started. For the first time it seemed to occur to her that the words were spoken with intention. Mr. Ash, who was still engaged upon his chin, did not appear to be able to go quite as far as his friend.

"That—eh—is perhaps a strongish thing to say—hardly crime—but it really does appear that blame rests somewhere—it really does."

But Mr. Ely was not to be gainsayed. No toning down of truths for him!

"I said, and I say again, that the person who is responsible for the bringing up of that young woman has committed a crime against society." He turned so that he looked Mrs. Clive straight in the face. "A girl is entrusted to her aunt to receive her education. If that aunt betrays her trust—miseducates the child! —then I challenge contradiction when I say that that aunt pulls away one of the props, the absence of whose support threatens to undermine the very fabric of society."

"Eh—there is—eh—of course one must admit that there is a certain substratum of truth in that."

"Is it possible"—smoothing the front of her dress with her two hands, it was evident that Mrs. Clive was awaking to the nature of the outrageous attack of which she was being made the victim—"is it possible that these remarks are directed against me?"

Thrusting his thumbs into his waistcoat armholes, Mr. Ely began to stride about the room.

"Oh, it's easy to throw about oneself the cloak of womanhood, and to claim that the privilege of sex exonerates from blame, but I should like to know, if this is to be the fate of the coming generation of young women, what will our future mothers be?"

Imitating Mr. Ely, Mr. Ash also thrust his thumbs into his waistcoat armholes.

"Just so! What will our future mothers be?"

"Our future mothers! Am I not a mother, then?"

But neither of the gentlemen paid the slightest attention to Mrs. Clive.

"It is not a question of our mothers only, it is a question of our fathers, too!"

"That is so. There can be no doubt that the maternal and paternal questions are closely intertwined."

"I never thought"—Mrs. Clive produced her handkerchief—"I never thought that I should have lived to see this day!"

Mrs. Clive began to cry; but neither of the gentlemen seemed at all abashed. They had a duty to perform, and evidently meant to carry it through.

"'Our acts our judges are, for good or ill.
Fatal shadows—which march by us still!'"

It was such an unusual thing for Mr. Ely to essay quotation that it was not surprising if the poet's words got slightly mangled in production. "The thing you do is like the seed you sow, it grows and grows until it assumes gigantic proportions, and blights your life and the lives of all whose paths you cross. You cannot get away from that!"

"You certainly cannot get away from that! That is well put—very well put, indeed!"

But Mrs. Clive was not to be trampled upon in silence. She turned on Mr. Ely with undaunted mien.

"May I ask, Mr. Ely, for an explanation of the language which you use?"

"Your niece, ma'am, is sufficient explanation. You say that what she is she owes to you. I presume her singular notions of morality among the rest!"

"Ahem!" Mr. Ash contented himself with clearing his throat.

"Mr. Ely, I am as much surprised at my niece's behaviour as you can possibly be."

"Surprised, madam! Why are you surprised? You say that you have handed on to her the precepts which you yourself imbibed at your mother's knee!"

"Sir!" Mrs. Clive turned towards Mr. Ash with her grandest air. "Mr. Ash, may I ask you to protect me from this gentleman?"

"I certainly understood you to say," stammered Mr. Ash, when he was thus appealed to, "that you had handed on to her the precepts which you had imbibed at your mother's knees?"

"Mr. Ash!" Up went the handkerchief to the injured lady's eyes.

"It's easy enough to cry," sneered Mr. Ely. "I believe that some people keep a stock of tears on hand. At the same time"—he turned on Mr. Ash with a sudden ferocity that was really startling—"don't suppose for a moment that I acquit you entirely from blame."

Mrs. Clive's tears were checked in the very act of starting to her eyes. Mr. Ash, about to move from the position in front of the fireplace which he had occupied until then, was apparently momentarily turned into stone. This sudden change of front seemed to take him very much aback.

"Oh, I know! I know!" continued Mr. Ely. "You may stare at me as much as you please, but I'm not to be frightened by your looks! I've not forgotten how you tried to rob me once before."

"This," exclaimed Mr. Ash, looking up, as though he apostrophised the skies, "is the most outrageous attack of which I ever heard!"

He had apparently forgotten that Mrs. Clive had just been the victim of a very similar attack in which he and his present antagonist had joined their forces.

"Bah!" cried Mr. Ely; "stuff and nonsense! Whenever there is any dirty work about I always see your hand. Who robbed me of a thousand pounds!"

"This," exclaimed Mr. Ash, extending his hands as though he were addressing an unseen audience, "is the man who robbed me of five hundred and thirty-three pounds thirteen and fourpence!"

Mr. Ely flung himself upon a seat and nursed his knee.

"If I had done what I ought to have done, I should have locked you up."

"Locked me up!" The words were gasped rather than spoken.

Mr. Ash turned to Mrs. Clive with the apparent intention of explaining to her the situation—it perhaps required explanation. "Madam, you see this man" ("this man" was the recent friend of his bosom, Frederic Ely), "he is so incapable of concealing his true character that even an inexperienced girl has found him out, and because she—very properly—refuses to have anything to do with him at any price, he turns on me! Madam," Mr. Ash became warmer as he spoke, "you are not acquainted with the intricacies of the Stock Exchange, but I think you will understand me when I tell you that I once sold him a quantity of a certain stock, and when there was a fall, so that there was a profit in my favour of five hundred and thirty-three pounds thirteen shillings, he had the audacity to say that I had bought, not sold, and he actually declared that the transaction had referred to double amount of the stock than was in reality the case, and he even preferred a claim against me for over a thousand pounds!"

"How shocking!" said Mrs. Clive. Though it may be suspected that she would have found it difficult to explain what was shocking if she had been required to do so on the spot.

Mr. Ely rose from his seat. He seemed more at his ease than he had been since he entered the room, as though falling out with Mr. Ash had relieved his mind.

"Ah," he observed, "that's the sort of man he is; if he robbed his mother he would swear that she'd robbed him. But perhaps he's not to blame. According to the new philosophy that sort of thing is in the blood."

Mr. Ash turned pale.

"Mrs. Clive, may I ask you to withdraw?"

"That's another of his dodges; he doesn't want you to know what sort of man he is. But I don't mind telling you, not the least. He's not the sort of man

I should care to choose to be trustee to my girl. He is the sort of man who regards a trusteeship as the royal road to wealth."

Mr. Ash began to grow angry, which was not surprising on the whole.

"Mrs. Clive, that man is the greatest thief in town."

"That's why he wanted me to marry his ward—that we might go halves, you know."

This remark so evidently enraged Mr. Ash that Mrs. Clive actually feared that hostilities would be commenced upon her drawing-room floor. She endeavoured to interpose.

"Gentlemen, I must beg of you to consider where you are!"

"You mustn't ask from him impossibilities; he can't realise that he's in a respectable house, you know."

Mr. Ash almost foamed at the lips.

"If you will not withdraw, Mrs. Clive, then in your presence I shall be compelled to thrash this man within an inch of his life."

"Gentlemen! I do beg of you!—I pray!"

"There's not the slightest occasion to be alarmed. Threatened men proverbially live long. Honest men know from experience that they can listen unmoved to the tall language used by the more doubtful members of society."

Mr. Ely ostentatiously jingled the money in his trouser pockets, and smiled a beatific smile.

"You hound!"

Mrs. Clive was in time to seize Mr. Ash's uplifted arm.

"Mr. Ash!" she cried.

"Hallo, Ash! What's the matter, Ash? Want to exhibit a little valour on the cheap?"

"You cur!"

Mr. Ash caught Mr. Ely by the collar, and Mr. Ely sprang at Mr. Ash's throat. The lady screamed. A very pretty fight was spoiled by the sudden appearance of other actors on the scene.

CHAPTER XVII

MR. ELY THROWS THE LADY OVER

"Guardian! Mr. Ely! What is the matter now?"

Miss Truscott and Mr. Summers were standing at the window. They had approached unperceived in the excitement of the little argument which had been taking place within. The lady's face was lighted with her sweetest, happiest smile. The gentleman, too, seemed at his ease; he had the lady's hand in his. The perfect agreement which evidently existed between the lovers was in striking contrast to the perfect disagreement which was conspicuous within. Outside the room, perfect peace; inside the room, a raging storm.

On the appearance of this united pair the combatants had the grace to let each other go. All signs of actual violence vanished into space. The old lady ceased to scream. Mr. Ash hastened to the window; his plumes were still a little ruffled.

"Lily, you have been better advised than I. I commend your choice. Rather than see you the wife of such a man as Frederic Ely, I would cut your throat."

Miss Truscott looked surprised. Mr. Ash's language was strong in an unexpected place. Mr. Summers laughed outright. Mr. Ely picked up his hat, which had been up to now reposing on a chair, and settled it upon his head.

"Mr. Summers, I can't congratulate you—I really can't. Not that I have anything to say against the lady—at least not much. But the man Ash—her guardian—is the most notorious character in town. Rather than become in any way connected with such a person as that I would march single to the silent grave. Good day, Mrs. Clive. I hope that Pompey continues in the enjoyment of good health."

Nodding slightly to Mrs. Clive, Mr. Ely swaggered from the room. Miss Truscott's look of surprise when he had gone was comical.

"Guardian, what does this mean?"

Mr. Ash still seemed a little uncomfortable, but he tried to pass it off as lightly as he could.

"Nothing, my dear, nothing. Let me beg of you to dismiss the incident wholly from your mind. Mr. Ely has revealed an unexpected phase in his character, but it was a phase which was better discovered early than late. I assure you that your engagement with my old friend Summers gives me complete content. May your days be happy and your love live long."

The lady looked her lover in the face.

"It will live long, I think."

"I am sure it will," said he.

They clasped each other by the hand; the old lady and the stockbroker turned away. There is a candour about true love which worldly minds find at times embarrassing.

Shortly afterwards the following announcement appeared in a daily paper

—

"Ely—Rosenbaum.—On the 6th instant, at St. Philip's, South Kensington, Frederic Ely, Esq., of the Stock Exchange, to Ruth, sixth and youngest daughter of Myer Rosenbaum, Esq., of Queen's Gate, S.W., and the Stock Exchange. No cards."

Miss Truscott showed this to Mr. Summers. They laughed together when they read it. Not many weeks elapsed before their names appeared in the same column of the *Times*.

Lightning Source UK Ltd.
Milton Keynes UK
UKHW042317030123
414627UK00018B/397

9 783752 416640